Praise for
JOHN D. MacDONALD
and
BARRIER ISLAND

"INGENUITY, EXPERIENCE, CRAFTSMAN-
SHIP, INTELLIGENCE—ALL OF THOSE ARE
HERE.... The procedural novel of American
business chicanery is peculiarly John D.
MacDonald's.... MacDonald is peerless in this
metier...a good read that will repay your
interest."

Chicago Sun-Times

"A pleasant way to be entertained...
MacDonald has an easy manner and a
marvelous ability to slip in little asides about
the amusing quirks of dogs, birds, humans,
and other creatures. He is able to define even
the minor characters in a few deft strokes."

St. Louis Post-Dispatch

(MORE)

JOHN D. MacDONALD

"I doubt whether Faulkner understood his Yoknapatawpha County any better than John D. MacDonald has the measure of the 'Redneck Riviera,' the stretch along the Gulf of Mexico from the Florida panhandle to the Texas border. People who haven't read MacDonald—and ought to—may think of it as *Body Heat* territory, but he invented it as a subject of art. Indeed, the popular film was pure MacDonald—without the credits.... This is the stuff to which MacDonald returns in BARRIER ISLAND in fighting trim...moves right along adroitly and insightfully, with a number of nicely individuated, well-sketched characters intertwining effectively...very worth reading...both a good story and some bitter food for thought."

The Washington Post Book World

BARRIER ISLAND

BARRIER ISLAND

"Prodigiously talented and prolific, MacDonald writes intelligent thrillers about the real world...unfolds the plot with the dramatic flair of a master storyteller...A novelist whose books have sold more than 70 million copies is not suspected of literary virtues, yet MacDonald is far more gifted than many of his peers who are taken more seriously...sketches the laid-back life of golf, boating, long cool drinks, the peculiar callousness bred of hot climates and luxurious comfort better than anybody since Graham Greene."

Los Angeles Times Book Review

JOHN D. MacDONALD

Other FAWCETT BOOKS
by John D. MacDonald

BARRIER ISLAND

John D. MacDonald

FAWCETT GOLD MEDAL • NEW YORK

A Fawcett Gold Medal Book
Published by Ballantine Books
Copyright © 1986 by John D. MacDonald Publishing, Inc.

All rights reserved under International and Pan-American Copyright Conventions. Published in the United States by Ballantine Books, a division of Random House, Inc., New York, and simultaneously in Canada by Random House of Canada Limited, Toronto.

Library of Congress Catalog Card Number: 85-45998

ISBN 0-449-13179-3

This edition published by arrangement with Alfred A. Knopf, Inc.

Manufactured in the United States of America

First Ballantine Books Edition: June 1987

To the memory of
Maxwell Penrose Wilkinson

In baiting a mouse trap with cheese,
always leave room for the mouse.

SAKI

 1

A night bird winging back to one of the islands made a harsh sobbing cry as it passed near a small cruiser anchored well to the south of the channel. The sound brought the owner up out of sleep, wrenching him out of his dreams into a moment of confusion before he sorted his world into the small realities of time and place.

He was naked on top of the sheets, sweaty, and with a thick headache somewhere behind his left brow. The sea was so still he could detect no motion, nor could he hear any slap of water against the fiberglass hull of the *Thelma III*. He heard a humming sound begin and knew it was the cooler. The woman in the other bunk made a thick snorting sound and settled back into her quiet sleep.

Loomis stood up and felt his way to the two steps and the hatch, and the cockpit deck. It was lighter under the invisible stars. Morning mist obscured them. Off to the east, toward Florida, was the first suggestion of dawn, a deep red line, narrow as a needle, along the watery edge of Mississippi Sound, out there close to infinity, close to the edge of the world where, if things were properly arranged, one could fall off. Or push someone off. Or hold hands and jump.

He felt around in the scuppers until he found his soggy red swimming trunks, discarded soon after he had jollied and cajoled Helen Yoder out of the black and white swimsuit he had loaned her. He stepped into the trunks and pulled them up. Didn't matter if there was no live person left on earth, a man felt better with a little bit of protection between his private possessions and the toothy creatures of the deep.

Tucker Loomis climbed heavily over the transom, stood on the small mahogany diving platform for a few moments, then sat and dangled his legs in the soup-warm sea, and slid in, glad of the chance to sluice away the sour sweat of hot night and too much to drink. The drinking seldom happened. It was not a problem. But the pressures were heavy lately. Have to keep watch for a correlation. If drinking goes up with the pressure, time to get back on the wagon. As he swam a slow circuit of his little cruiser, he emptied his bladder into the summer sea, heat into warmth. A notable example of environmental pollution. Get the professors all agitated and jumpy about it. They'd probably say that ten months and three days from now they could scoop up a pan of water in Sydney Harbor and take it to the lab and find one part in forty trillion is hangover piss out of old Tuck Loomis, one of the great despoilers of

God's own earth. With some real sophisticated procedures maybe they could find out that this pleasant pee at dawn had originated in a couple of bottles of the best champagne put out by Perrier. Maybe eighty dollars a pop in your best restaurant. Pretty flowers on the bottle. That old senator surely went for it in a big way last April in New Orleans in the suite.

He circled the boat three times, and when he climbed back aboard, the narrow red line was a broad pink band, and there was less mist overhead. He stepped out of the trunks, picked them up and wrung them out and spread them along the back of the fishing chair to dry.

When he went below to get a fresh towel, Helen yoder was sitting up in her bunk, arms wrapped around her legs, forehead on her knees. She raised her head and glanced at him and lowered it again. Her dark blonde hair was a wild tangle.

"And a cheery good morning to you too, little buddy," he said.

"Just shut up, Tuck. Okay?"

"That bad?"

She did not answer. He knelt and took a towel out of the stowage locker under her bunk. Enough gray light came through the small port to make a silver glow on the bunk behind her and toweled the mat of wiry gray on his chest and the thick crop of white hair on his broad skull. He leaned forward, pawed her hair out of the way and gave her a noisy kiss on the nape of the neck.

She flinched, swung around and sat the other way

3

on the bunk and pulled the sheet across her lap. "No. No thanks."

"That was just for good morning, that's all."

Her face was in shadow. The gray of predawn made a moist highlight on the curve of her left breast. "Where are we, Tuck? Back at the dock?"

"We're way out on the sandy flats, honey. Ten miles about. Half a mile off Bernard Island. Flat calm."

She combed her tangled hair back with the splayed fingers of both hands. "Jesus, Tucker! This is dumb. What if Buddy phoned last night, or this morning even?"

"Why should he all of a sudden phone *you*? You told me last night he's been staying at his sister's place for a month. And you told me he's up in Washington this week."

She frowned at him. "I told you all that? Well . . . I guess I remember. What more did I tell you?"

"People are forever telling me all kinds of stuff. I listen good, sweetie. I like people. I really do. I like to listen to the problems they got. Everybody's got problems."

"Anyway, this is Friday and I've got to go to the office. And my car's at the club! I'm going to be pretty damn conspicuous trying to get to my car from the dock. In my long blue dress."

"There's some stuff aboard should fit you okay. good as the swimsuit did. T-shirts, shorts. Under that other bunk. You can dig around in there, see what you find. Feel free. Nobody to see you but some early morning tennis freaks."

"Look, can we get started back?"

4

"Not yet."

"Why not?"

"Honey, how long is it since we had us like they call it, a relationship? Three years? Four?"

"Let me see. How long has Cordell been dead? Then it would be more like five years ago, Tuck. We started a month after he hit that tree. And we were together the best part of a year."

"Then you should remember, little buddy, how pissed I get when people keep asking me fool questions. Just you relax."

The small cruiser stirred suddenly, lifting and rolling in the slow swell from a distant barge train going up the waterway. It settled slowly back to stillness, but it had swung far enough on the anchor line to bring the morning light against her face. Smudge of lipstick, smear of mascara. It was a handsome and vital face, with large features, a strong jawline and brow. But it bore the lines and folds of her thirty-five years.

"I'm a mess," she said. "I feel rotten. I haven't had that much wine in years. You woke me up sloshing around out there. I think a swim is probably a pretty good idea for starters. Okay? But you keep an eye on me. I don't like to swim way out here without somebody watching out."

The sun came up as she was swimming back and forth behind the transom, about thirty feet each way like someone in a small swimming pool instead of in the endless serenity of the Sound. She climbed out and sat on the transom and scrubbed her face and her teeth with a wet corner of the towel he handed her.

"Better get below and fix yourself up," he said.

"Are we heading in?"

"You go on down. I'll be there in a minute and tell you what's going to happen, Helen. And what you have to do."

"What's going on?"

He sighed. "Just shut up and move it."

He put on old khaki pants and a torn white shirt. Their good clothes were in the hanging locker. When he went below she was fixing her face. She had brushed her hair, and picked out a pink shirt and white shorts spotted with green paint, and he recognized them as a pair one of his daughters-in-law had left aboard long ago.

"Okay, here's what's going to come down, as they say on the television. A man is going to meet me out here in the next ten or fifteen minutes. He's coming in a float plane. He's a very careful man. The deal was just him and me and the pilot, but I don't like that setup. I'm supposed to be out here by myself. I decided I better have company."

She stared at him, her eyes narrowing. "Oh dear God! And all the time I was thinking this was some kind of sentimental journey. Kind of a sweet idea, on account of the real good times we used to have together. Tuck, you miserable son of a bitch! You are the *worst*!"

"I guess you could call it an impulse."

"If it was all planned out, it's some funny kind of impulse. Tell me about it."

"What I thought I'd do, I was going to tell Mike Wasser to come along."

"Who's he?"

"He works for me. Big fella. Hell of a linebacker at State. Anyway, I hadn't phoned him yet to show up at the club, and I was sitting there at the corner of the bar and you came walking by in your blue dress and I thought you'd be a lot more fun than Mike. And you were, up until just now when you started fussing."

He watched her decide how she was going to react. He remembered those two deep little vertical lines which appeared between her brows when she was selecting the right part to play. She laughed and shook her head. "You are something," she said. "You are really rotten. Okay. What do I do?"

"You can keep right on doing what you're doing until the seaplane lands, which won't be long now. I'm going to leave this hatch door open so he can see right down into here and see it's empty. I want you all scrunched up at the foot end of this port bunk, all the way out of sight. Not a sound out of you. And sooner or later I'll call to you and then you come on up on deck. Smile sweet at him. His name is Wilbur Barley and he works for the government, and he is going to be a little pissed. Just play it by ear from there on in. You're a smart lady, and I'm glad it's you on board instead of Mike."

He heard the seaplane before he saw it. The sun was above the horizon and the mist was burned away. The sea was the color of lead, hinting of blue to come. A flurry of bait sparkled in the sunshine as something made a pass at it, scaring it into the air. He waved as the aircraft circled the boat, then moved away and turned and came toward him, skimming, touching,

7

landing, taxiing close. Tuck was amused to see that the I.D. numbers on the plane were covered with tape. Barley was cautious.

Barley climbed down onto the port pontoon. Tuck threw him a line and they pulled the two vessels close enough for Barley to step onto the platform and climb onto the transom and jump down into the cockpit. The aircraft pulled away and the pilot cut the engine, making the morning a lot quieter.

"How you been?" Tuck asked.

"You bring it?" Wilbur Barley asked. He was a pale puffy man in his thirties, with blonde hair combed forward, a small blonde mustache, glasses with thin gold rims. This was the third time Loomis had seen the man. The other two times, in Biloxi, Wilbur Barley had worn a pale gray three-piece suit, white shirt, blue tie, shiny black moccasins with brass buckles. Now he looked unlikely in his white slacks and running shoes, in his green short-sleeved shirt with a gator on the left breast—out of sync in time and space, like a piece of miscasting in an amateur play.

Loomis stuck his hand out and, grinning, left it there until Barley had to take it. Tuck shook the soft white hand and said, "Hey, you set yourself down, man. Right here. Let me get these swim pants out of the way. We're not in all that big a hurry, are we?"

"Listen, I don't want to be seen here, Mr. Loomis. You can understand that."

"By who? That there gull? Or a fish maybe. The charter boys won't be starting out until about now, so it'll be a half hour anyway before we see one heading this way."

"Mr. Loomis, are you stalling because you weren't able to bring it?"

"Why wouldn't I be able to bring it?"

"Well, it *is* a lot of money."

Tuck was amused at the innocence and the slyness of the man, at the naked attempt to find out just how much the money meant to him.

"I guess anybody could call half of it a pretty good piece of money."

"Half is not acceptable."

"Now why wouldn't it be?"

"Because to get the other half we would have to arrange to meet one more time. And once is quite enough risk. I think we better call this whole thing off right now."

Loomis sighed and went over to the wheel and unlocked the flat drawer below the instrument panel. He took out the thick, heavy mailing envelope and flipped it onto Barley's lap. Barley slapped at it and caught it before it fell to the deck.

"Half," Loomis said. "In hundreds. I'm not a total damn fool, in spite of what a lot of people will try to tell you. If that little old seaplane falls out of the sky on the way home, I'm only half as sorry. If you find out you just can't do what you allowed you could do, then we dicker about how much of that you give back."

"Give back!" Barley said, shocked. "I'm taking a terrible risk with my career, and the risk is the same whether it works out or not."

"One thing for sure. If it doesn't work out, you don't get the other half. And if it does, you'll get the rest in a nice safe easy way. No sweat and no strain. And we'll most probably never see each other again."

Barley lifted the tape on the envelope flap and looked inside. Tucker Loomis felt the inner relaxation. The look of the money always makes the deal. And he noticed that Barley swiveled the fishing chair just enough to turn his back toward the waiting seaplane before he looked into the envelope at the two bulky packets.

"I don't like this," Barley said.

"Wilbur, most people feel a little edgy about taking a risk. We're both clear on what you're going to do. You're going to make damn well sure the U.S. Attorney's Office fumbles the ball real good when we come to trial."

"I'm going to *try* to make sure. It isn't an easy thing to do, to make it look as if it . . . just happened that way."

"You do your best, hear? Helen, honey! Come on out and meet somebody."

He watched Barley's face as Helen, ducking to clear the upper part of the frame, came up out of the hatch, smiling.

"Honey, this is Mr. Wilbur Barley and he works for—"

Barley was on his feet, no color left in his face. "I told you to be alone, dammit! What are you trying to pull, you son of a bitch?"

"I don't like being called names, Wilbur. It upsets me a lot."

"I'm pretty upset too, Mr. Loomis."

"You can trust Helen here. You don't have to worry about her."

"I didn't want to have to worry about anybody but you."

"And that would leave two of you for me to worry on."

"Oh, that's my sister's husband flying the plane."

"And your sister knows about this too I suppose."

"She's been in a coma for over a year."

"I'm sorry to hear that."

"She fell in the bathtub and hit her head. It's a terrible expense. I wouldn't have gotten into this if . . . But I guess you don't give a damn about my motives."

"Well, I did wonder why a man with your reputation for being a straight arrow would be willing to deal. It's comforting to know you haven't got in the habit of flying off to Vegas or Atlantic City."

Barley stared at Helen and then at Loomis. He glanced at the rail and Loomis knew that for an instant the thought had crossed Barley's mind that it might be a good idea to toss the package overboard in a gesture of despair. He looked strangely close to tears. "You promised you'd be alone!"

Loomis smiled broadly at him. "I guess I lied. You don't have to worry about Helen. She's just here in case you decide sometime to swear you were never here at all. That's all. She's just a precaution, isn't that right, little lady?"

"If you say so, Tuck. Glad to meet you, Mr. Barley."

He stared at her for ten long seconds and then nodded. He pulled his green shirt out of his slacks, laid the mailer against his plump belly and tucked the shirt in again.

"Just don't try to get in touch with me in any way until the trial is over. Is that quite clear?"

"Don't use that prosecuting attorney tone of voice on me, Wilbur. Just call your brother-in-law and fly away."

Tuck and Helen Yoder stood side by side and watched the little seaplane skim and roar and lift, then make a shallow turn and head northwest by west.

The water was turning blue, and a breeze ruffled the surface. The mainland was invisible under smog and clouds. Heavy weather by nightfall. The marine forecast had been right on. He slid his thick hand down Helen's back, and gave the far buttock a hearty, honking squeeze.

"Hey!" she said, and sprang away from him. "I've really got to go to work today. I've got appointments."

"Every little love pat, you think I'm about to jump you."

"That's the way you always used to be."

"But now I'm fifty-damn-eight years old."

"Can we go now? Please?"

"Get your cute ass up there on the bow and bring in the anchor line as I run up on it. If it don't come free, take a turn around—"

"Just like I've done a couple thousand times before."

He started the inboard-outboards as she went forward. As he eased up toward the hook, he realized how pleased he was with Wilbur Barley's reaction.

Right from the first contact, there had been the possibility that they were trying to set him up. Bribing a federal officer. A pilot with a telephoto lens. But little ol' chubby Wilbur had come through like a champion. Helen's sudden appearance had been the stress test. Because, had it been a trap, Barley would have realized at once that the woman could give false information in an affidavit that would cause the jaws of the trap to snap shut on air. Wilbur would have had to be a first-class theatrical actor to handle it the way he did.

And, in addition to his help this time, you never knew when you might like to have somebody well placed in Wilbur's spot for anything else that might come up in the future. There were people here and there in Jackson and Biloxi and Washington who had come to like doing favors for Tuck Loomis and having favors done in return. That was the way you got to sit in the owner's box to watch the game.

He saw Helen lean and lift the hook out of the water, careful to keep it away from the hull. She lifted the small forward hatch and stowed it. When she stepped back down into the cockpit, he pushed both throttles forward and when the boat was on the plane, he pulled the throttles back and balanced them off at twenty-eight hundred.

She stood beside him, a hand on his shoulder. "I suppose I shouldn't ask what that was all about, huh?" She had to lean close to him and speak loudly over the engine roar.

"You suppose exactly right."

"It's the condemnation on Bernard Island, isn't it?"

"I don't like smartass women."

13

"Like you told that Barley, you can trust old Helen."

He smiled up at her. "I sure can, little buddy. If I didn't have a good lock on you, you wouldn't have been out here at all."

"What kind of a lock?"

"I don't mean I've got something I can hold over your head. It's just that we had a good time together and we parted friends and stayed friends. Okay? You're my buddy, aren't you? My old pal?"

"I guess so. Sure. Why not?"

"You don't sound all eager and happy."

"Should I? Hell, I don't know. My life doesn't seem to go anyplace at all lately. Not since Cordell died."

Every time she mentioned his death, her mind slipped back into the same old groove, like a repeating track worn in a record. Cordell Strange had been hurrying back home to her from a meeting in Gulfport, and going so damned fast in a light rain in that stupid TransAm he was outrunning his headlights. And he came upon a big dead dog in his lane that someone else had hit. He swerved and lost it and went a hundred feet off the highway before he smashed head-on into an old cypress. Somebody had phoned in to have the dog pulled off the road, and when a state policeman got there and got out of his car he heard the tape still playing in the TransAm and he went looking and found Cordell in the car, all crushed and dead.

She examined all of it every time it went through her head. If only this. If only that. If only the other thing.

"I shouldn't get sour with you, Tuck. I guess you

were good for me. I needed *somebody.* Everything in the world turned so flat, you know? You were very sweet and I appreciated it. Of course, you can be mean as a snake too. But I don't know, I think when Cordell hit the tree I lost my luck. It wasn't a good move to marry Buddy Yoder. I think you tried to tell me that, Tuck."

"All I think I told you, if I remember, I kindly told you that Hubbard Yoder, Attorney at Law, ain't too playful."

"Well, it's over. He doesn't think it is but it is. I don't know what's wrong with me. I'm doing pretty good. I'm making money. This afternoon I'm showing the old Crown house to some people who want to turn it into one of those bed and breakfast places, very elegant, like the best in England. I've worked up all the figures on it and I know what they have to come up with to make it bankable, and I worked up all the expenses they'll run into including the rezoning, and I had Jeanie run off a pie chart on the PC. It's very nice-looking. I think I've got a good chance. This is the third time I'll have been over it with them. They want to dicker the commission, but there's a place I won't go lower than. I figure I'll net ten or eleven thousand out of the deal, and I bet I've put in a hundred hours on that sucker so far. I have some leverage on them because I had them put up five hundred nonreturnable on a two-month option so nobody would steal it out from under them, and I had one hell of a job talking old Mrs. Crown's legal guardian into taking such small money. Hey, I'm getting hoarse yelling at you, Tuck.

And you don't want to hear all this dreary stuff anyway. Who's that coming?"

"Looks like Jersey Joe in the *African Queen*. Yeah. He'll be going fifty or sixty miles out working red snapper. Even if he's into a million of them, another boat shows on the horizon, he pulls up and moves. Joe don't share. He's got eight stations for those big electric reels of his."

"So excuse me," she said and went below.

They passed close enough to wave. Soon the mainland shore was in view, and Loomis made a course correction to hit the markers at the mouth of Alden Bay and the Alden River. His most successful residential housing development was six miles up the river. Parklands, a two-thousand-acre complex northeast of West Bay. He went up the narrow channel dead slow against the current, enjoying the look of the old trees with the beards of moss, the gentle roll of the countryside, the children of summer playing in the river and on the lawns. He liked the summer smell of the land, a hot and slightly acrid fragrance. His headache was gone.

Soon he was inside Parklands, heading for the yacht club, passing the elegant homes on both sides of the river. Gate guards, large lots, golf course, country club, tennis courts. He was comfortably aware of the five hundred acres of land not yet subdivided and marketed. Money in the bank. Parklands was the best address within miles of West Bay. All the bankers and lawyers and doctors and politicians. Fred Pittman and Colonel Barkis had been in with him on that one, right from the beginning. Big plans. Big loans. It had started strong and then after the first year it began to stall out. And the interest had begun to eat them up.

Fred and the Colonel had lost their confidence in the Parklands project. They kept at him all the time about spending too much money. But he knew it would work. And he wished he had the money to buy them out. He tried to borrow it. He tried to talk them into taking his personal notes. But then the project began to pick up, began to move, began to prove itself out. He had learned to handle his deals by himself from then on. Except, of course, when you wanted to cut somebody into something nice, just as a favor for a good friend.

At the weekly poker sessions with Pink Derks, Sam Loudner, Woodrow Daggs, Warner Ellenson, Fred Pittman and the Colonel, he could detect a new quality of cordiality and respect, quite unlike the coolness he had sensed when it looked to the others—but not to him—as though Parklands was going down the big tube. He enjoyed the change of attitude. He had been the new boy in the group, a little bit out of place with the men representing the biggest bank, the biggest construction company, the biggest law firm and the political structure. But Parklands bought him his legitimate membership, and they had begun to solicit his opinions on local development and the probable direction of the population expansion.

Smiling to himself, he eased the *Thelma III* into her slip, cut the engines and tossed the lines to the boy who came running down from the dockmaster's office.

 2

The Monday morning staff meeting at Rowley/Gibbs Associates was over by ten-fifteen. After their people had filed out, Wade Rowley stayed in Bern Gibbs' big corner office, behind the closed door, after sending Dawn Marino, Bern's secretary, back out to her desk.

Bern sat at his big slab desk, chair tilted back, fingers laced at the nape of his neck, heels propped on the desk corner. The collar of his white shirt was unbuttoned, his tie pulled down. He was a lean man with a narrow face and a sailor's tan. He had thick black hair brushed back to cover the top half of his ears, and trained to loop across his forehead to hide the receding hairline. His eyes were a bright and startling green. Except for a recent thickness around the middle, he looked fit. His sleeves were rolled halfway up his wiry, hairy forearms.

"That Beth's red toyota out there?" Bern asked.

"The air quit yesterday and the wear on the front left is bad, cupping the tire. So Wally will pick it up and get it back here by five." Wade sat in the secretarial chair at the end of the desk, where Dawn always sat to take notes on the meeting. Wade Rowley was a big fair-skinned man with a bland, stolid, mid-American face, a John Denver face. His light brown hair was habitually tousled, combed forward into an uneven fringe of bangs. His eyes were brown. He moved slowly and often looked sleepy. Today he wore a white guayabera and blue seersucker slacks. He rested his forearms on the end of the desk. "Not too bad of a report for the middle of July, partner."

"I like that Yoder sale on the Crown place. If it goes through okay."

"A hundred thousand earnest money in front indicates sincerity," Wade said. "And like Helen said, she's been working on it for months, doing the research they should have done. I've talked to them twice. If they work at it, they'll make some money. But I get the feeling they're not going to cut it. They've both always worked for other people and their wives haven't worked at all. More restaurants go broke than anything else in the world."

Bern yawned. "We don't have to worry about it. We get ours out of the front money. Let the bank sweat it."

"I'll worry. Because I always worry about things like that. I'll see them on the street and I'll worry. And what's new with you?"

"Funny thing. I had lunch Saturday with Bill

Glover. We're the entertainment committee for the Lions this coming year. He lives out there at Parklands. He and Hilda get in a lot of early tennis. Okay, they were playing Friday morning and the court they were on isn't too far from the yacht club docks. He saw Tuck Loomis' little boat come in. Tuck tied it up and then he walked around to the parking area and pretty soon he showed up again back near the dock in an old blue and white Chevy van. And pretty soon Helen Yoder came scrambling out of the boat with some kind of blue clothes over her arm, popped into the van and yelped the tires in a big hurry to get out of there. Didn't they used to see a lot of each other?"

"For a little while, I think. Back before she married Buddy. Not long after Cordell got himself killed. What are you getting at?" Wade asked.

"I don't know. Bill said it was kind of a sneaky scene."

Wade shrugged. "They're grown-up people. Buddy and Helen are separated. Tuck is a stud. He and Helen probably ran into each other at that Thursday night benefit at the Parklands Yacht Club, had a couple of drinks and took a boat ride."

Bern sighed and said, "If it wasn't, like they say, too close to the flagpole, I'd like to get me some of that. The young kids are too jumpy. Ol' Helen looks like she'd settle right down to it. A real worker." Bern stared at Wade and then shook his head and laughed. "I talk like that and you always get that look on your face. You some kind of prude, partner?"

"Only when it comes down to the people working for us."

"So pardon me all to hell."

"Who was it came up with the plan to get Mrs. Karp out of that condo?"

"Tom Hatchuk told me it was Joyce's idea. Everybody has been trying to solve the woman's problem. Mrs. Karp's deal is one of the reasons we fired Chuck. He shoved her in there way over her head. So Joyce said maybe Freedom Federal would deal. She owed eighty on it. Tom went to Al Wescowitz at Freedom and asked him what he'd take in cash to get out of it, and dickered him down to sixty-eight thousand, with a cancellation of the back interest. Then Tom went to Mr. Knight, told him he had a good tenant lined up, told him the new price, and Knight bought it on spec for seventy-five cash money. Freedom got paid off and Mrs. Karp got off the hook. Because this agency got her into that mess, we swallowed the commission."

"Tom too?"

"One thousand for creative thinking. Plus he makes a little off the rental. But if it's okay with you, I want to give Joyce Kindred a little bonus for a good idea."

"I think we should."

"You know, Wade, these Monday meetings make me kind of uneasy."

"You keep telling me that."

"I don't want to stop them. They keep everybody in touch with what the others are doing. A lot of good ideas get bounced around. But you never handle the meeting."

"You're good at it."

"Okay, pal, we each own half the stock in this here Chapter S corporation, and here I am with the big corner office, and I handle the meeting and I sign the paychecks."

"And it works fine, doesn't it?"

"Sometimes I get a little pissed. You sit over there in the corner and keep your mouth shut, and when somebody brings something up they're not sure they should, they beat around the bush and they keep glancing over at you to see how you're taking it. If you start frowning they back off, and if you give one of those little nods of yours, then they charge ahead. I mean I'm handling the meeting but I'm not in charge."

"We're both in charge, Bern. Sometimes I veto you and sometimes you veto me. That's why it works out okay."

"That's why it used to work out."

This, Wade knew, was uncomfortable ground, to be traversed with great care. "I think we've both been a little bit tense lately."

"Just tell me one time when I vetoed you."

"On the Bernard Island deal."

"That was over a year ago."

"And I still think we made a mistake."

"It was a nice little gold mine while it lasted. Tell me what's wrong."

"Yesterday morning early I went out with Tod in the Whaler after specs. Flat calm. We worked the grass flats out near Petit Bois and did pretty good, and then as the sun got higher and the tide changed, they stopped biting."

"How's Tod doing?"

"He's enjoying being sixteen. Says it is a *lot* older than fifteen. And he's catching up okay in summer school. Anyway, I decided we could take a look at Bernard Island. We pulled the Whaler up on the sand at the west end and we waded all the way around the island. Well, not all the way. It drops off pretty deep out there at the southeast by the old high dunes, so we went ashore and walked by that part. We found a lot of the stakes Tuck's surveyors put in. Galvanized pipe with a red ribbon streamer on the top, and lot numbers in black paint on the side of the pipe. Lot of bugs out there, Bern. And a lot of lonesome. So quiet all you could hear was all those bugs and peepers shrilling away. How many lots were actually deeded?"

"Let me make sure." Bern opened the middle drawer of his desk and took out a yellow legal pad. He leafed back through several pages. "Here we are. Seventy-four. That doesn't mean that many buyers. Almost all of them took two half-acre lots."

"What's the most expensive one we've processed?"

"Two hundred and ten thousand for a full acre. A high piece, near the marina."

"Got the total so far?"

"Five-point-one-eight mil. Which at one-and-a-half percent negotiated commission is seventy-seven thousand seven hundred dollars for this splendid organization called Rowley/Gibbs Associates."

"I stood there in warm water halfway to my knees, Bern, and I looked north and I couldn't see any part of the mainland. Not any part of it. And then I thought about water supply, sewage disposal, fire and police protection, dumb stuff like that. And I thought about the dredging that would have to happen before barges loaded with building supplies could get close enough to

23

unload onto the island. I thought about grocery shopping and health care and all the permissions Loomis would have to get. Don't you think about things like that? Ever?"

"Every time I read one of those big think pieces in the *Courier Journal* by your old pal Brud Barnes. Otherwise not too often, partner. Developers are visionaries. They take big risks to make big profits. Name of the game, isn't it? Listen, Tuck has good contacts with a lot of rich people here and in Florida and Alabama and Louisiana. Rich people like seclusion. There'll be a little airstrip and a helicopter pad on the island. He's going to use some kind of new Swedish waste disposal system. He's going to generate his own electric. All those things are his problems, not ours. A lot of people thought Parklands was a bad idea. Look at it now. He's a responsible man, Wade. He's done a lot for this area."

"I've got some more questions."

"It figures. I've heard them before, right?"

"He has qualified people working for him. He's got his own broker's license. He could have processed all these deeds. How come he made us a gift of seventy-seven thousand?"

"I guess his people were busy on other things. Or he didn't want to be bothered."

"If those buyers are so rich, why did they pay him such tiny little down payments?"

"Didn't you read the fine print? Interest and mortgage payments start when all the required permits have been granted, and the first phase of road construction starts. If the project can't be started, the

24

down payments are returned with ten percent interest."

"What exactly did Dawn do on these deeds?"

"Tuck's office sent me a fact sheet for every purchase. Name, address, lot number, price, down payment, mortgage terms and so on. We put the deeds on disk, and Dawn filled in the data in between the boilerplate. She ran the required copies, and they went back to Tuck's office. His notary verified the signatures. They came back here and Dawn went down and recorded them, and in the next couple of days they would show up in the news of record."

"With our name?"

"We're the real estate agency involved."

"Not very involved."

"How involved can you get for one-point-five percent?"

"How did we get the commission?"

"In the mail. A check drawn on Loomis Development and sometimes on the Bernard Island Corporation."

"And we're the agency of record."

"Don't keep saying it and making it sound so sinister, for God's sake."

"Listen, we started fourteen years ago. Just the two of us in that phone-booth office in the old West Bay Citizens Bank building. Now we've got eight full-time employees, plus those part-timers Frank Mettler works with. A clean operation, Bern. We haven't had to tuck ourselves under the wing of one of the national franchises. We're a class act. Sometimes things get a little thin, but we always make out somehow. I'm not crazy about this arrangement."

"I know you aren't. You keep telling me. That's why we had Rick Riker check it all out. He's happy with it."

"You mean he couldn't find anything particularly wrong with it."

"When he can't find anything wrong, he's happy, isn't he?"

"That island is inside the West Bay County limits, and I tell you there is *no* way he could have gotten the county and state permits."

"When they added Bernard to the Gulf Islands National Seashore, then the whole thing about permits became academic, Wade."

"And this is where I say *Aha!*"

"I don't exactly follow you."

"Just when did Tuck Loomis find out they were going to take over that particular barrier island and add it to the rest of them?"

"When everybody else did, I guess. When it was announced. Last month. When the Park Service began condemnation. That put a stop to all sales and development. That's when they put seven hundred thousand in escrow as payment for Tuck's island."

"When did Tuck start planning the development?"

"Hmmm. Maybe two years ago."

"Isn't it worth seventy-seven thousand to make a land scam look a little more legitimate? Hell, we both know what he paid the Campana family for it."

"Half a million dollars."

"Ten thousand down and a note for the balance."

26

"What are you getting at, Wade, dammit? Look what he paid for all that raw land he turned into Parklands."

"And look at the amount of money he put into it out there, Bern! He and Colonel Barkis and Fred Pittman. Let me tell you a couple of things they can use to lift our license to do business, Bern. Employing an unlicensed salesman. Who exactly is selling these lots? Collecting an illegal commission. Did you ever hear of one-and-a-half percent for paperwork? Filing false instruments. Are these legitimate sales, or part of a scam? Conspiracy to defraud. Defraud who? The government?"

Bern jumped up, scowling. "Honest to Christ, Wade. You get to be more of an old lady every year. Riker checked it out. He didn't bring up any of that stuff. Thanks to Tuck Loomis, we had a damn good year, and we'll be able to stuff nice money into the Keoghs. And here's something I haven't told you. Tuck told me that when it comes time to open up that final five hundred acres at the Parklands, he might let us handle it. Do some of your damn arithmetic on that!"

"When did he tell you that?"

"I don't know. Last year maybe."

"Way back when he wrote you the letter asking us to handle the mortgage deeds?"

"I guess so."

"And that's what made you so hot to trot. Why did he pick us, Bern?"

"Maybe he likes the way we do business."

"Tuck likes money, women and bourbon, in that order."

"Do you think he was kidding me?"

"I think he was encouraging you to not look too close at these Bernard Island mortgage deeds."

"I'm not some innocent kid!" Bern shouted and sat down again, so hard that his chair rolled back and thumped against the mural of the county map on the wall behind his desk.

"I don't want some big scuffle about this," Wade said. "All I want you to do is think about it. And if you decide that maybe, just maybe, our necks are out, and that something might come out at the condemnation proceedings that could hurt us, you write me a detailed letter about why we shouldn't have gotten into this thing, and I will write you one, seconding your opinion, and those letters will go in the file and we will have something to produce if we have to, something besides a confession of greed."

"You are worrying too much. It's over. We did it and collected the money, and no more is coming in, not from that arrangement. It's over, Wade. So ease up on it, will you?"

"Nothing like that is ever over. Not when it's in the records. Not when it looks funny. So let's at least try to cover ourselves with the letters to each other. And put in yours the verbal promise he made about the five hundred acres he's going to open up at Parklands."

"No way."

"I convinced you we ought to get out of the bank and build this building three years ago. And they've been bumping the rent at the bank ever since."

"Mark up one for you."

"And I talked you into hiring Frank Mettler."

"And I *still* don't like the son of a bitch, but he sure can produce."

"We've got a good team. And don't think they don't know we've taken in a nice net on commissions for doing practically nothing. At least the smart ones know, and that includes Helen Yoder. She asked me about it months ago. I told her it was your account. I suppose she asked you and the answers didn't satisfy her, so maybe she let Tuck pick her up Thursday night because she wanted to ask him what the hell is going on. She has a good nose for something a little bit off. He's lost the island, right? Those buyers stand to get their little down payments back with interest. The recorded deeds will be canceled out. Without us in the picture, Bern, without an outlay of seventy-seven thousand dollars commissions on sales, the rest of it would look pretty thin. And the money he paid us will be in the statement he will produce at the condemnation trial, along with what he has paid engineers, architects, lawyers, model-makers, botanists, marine biologists and God knows who else. He can show that he *could* sell seventy-six acres for five plus million and *did* sell those acres, and if the Park Service hadn't spoiled the party, he would have had another couple of hundred to sell. We can be called in to testify. How are we going to look?"

"Just fine. Wade, you've got to realize we're living in the age of six-hundred-dollar toilet seats and three-thousand-dollar hex socket wrenches. If Tuck has found a way to get something for nothing out of the government, more power to him. We're doing nothing illegal."

"How about immoral?"

"You can worry about that, if you've got the time."

"Where are those data sheets you mentioned?"

"Dawn's got the file."

"Mind if I look them over?"

Bern Gibbs waved a casual hand. "You own half the action around here, buddy." Wade Rowley started toward the door. "Wait a minute," Bern said and came to stand in front of him. "I don't like fussing about this. I don't like the feeling you give me that I'm naive about Tucker Loomis and Bernard Island, and you are so wise and so sound. I've asked around. The general feeling among the developers and bankers and lawyers is that if anybody could have made out developing that six-hundred-acre island, ol' Tuck could. He bought it. The title was good. It was his. He could have gone to live in those old Campana shacks at the east end if he wanted to."

"They've been torched. Tod found an old anchor sitting in the charcoal."

"I didn't know that. Anyway, what he paid for it doesn't have a lot to do with what it's worth. You have to add in Tuck's vision of what it could become. Creative value added. And why should we argue about a nice piece of business? We'd have to sell a million-dollar building to make that much. Suppose it *is* some kind of a scam, Wade. What difference does it make? Our skirts are clean. We've got that letter from Tuck, his original proposal. We performed a service for a fee. Why do you get so damned nervous about things?"

Wade shrugged. "I guess it's the way I am."

When Wade got back to his own small office Brud Barnes was sitting on a corner of his desk, leafing through a copy of *Real Estate Today*. He was as tall as Wade, but not as heavy through the chest and shoulders. He had a narrow face, amber brown eyes that tilted down at the outside corners, big ears, beaver teeth, and thinning dark hair. He wore khakis, a white shirt, a faded baseball cap.

As he tossed the magazine back onto the desk, Wade said, "Either you want to borrow money or go fishing. It can't be in your line of work because I'm not what you call newsworthy."

"Been so long, I thought I'd make it a social call. But if you want to force money or fishing on me . . ."

"Fishing, sure. Any time."

They had grown up on the same street. And the years of running and battling and fishing had turned them into close friends. They both liked the outdoors, the woods and the water and the silences, and the creatures therein. They were both interested in conservation, but Brud's position as executive editor on the West Bay *Courier Journal*, one of the very few independent daily papers still operating on the Mississippi coast, and operating very profitably, gave him the chance to be effective.

They had served on many committees together, signed the same petitions, enjoyed a few minor victories and suffered more than a few major setbacks.

"How's Beth and the kids?"

"Chugging along pretty good. Tod had to do summer school this year. He faded in the stretch in the regular term."

"You and I did that once."

"I hate to remember that damn summer. I really do. How are you making out, Brud?"

"Keeping busy."

There had been a time when Brud's pleasant inquiry about Wade's family would have brought about a query about Alice and Sissy. But they were two years gone, living in Austin, Texas, with the lawyer Alice had married after she divorced Brud. Wade thought of all the others in their high-school class who'd been married and divorced. It was a small plague which had struck heavily in that age group in West Bay. And now it was infecting Helen and Buddy Yoder.

"I haven't seen you in over six months. I sent you a note about how much I like those three articles you've been doing on the islands."

"But I didn't answer, I guess. Busy or lazy. Probably lazy. Thanks anyway. I kind of bore down on Tuck Loomis and his plans for Bernard Island."

"Get any response?"

"Nobody walked in and shot me in the city room. And Parklands hasn't been running enough advertising lately so that it was worth it to them to pull it out. I run into him at the Hyatt one time over a month ago and he gave me that crookedy grin of his and said, 'Brud, baby, you never gone win any Pulitzer with that kinda shit.' So I asked him for something useful I could print, like how long had he known that the feds were going to pick up Bernard Island. He gave me his wide-eyed-innocence look and he said, 'You musta knowed before I did.' It gripes my ass the way he comes on so grits and syrup these days. The son of a bitch come down here from Ohio. He thinks he's one of the boys, in with them close and tight, boys like Derks and Ellenson and Loudner. But they're just jollying him because he's making a little money for them here and there, and they do love that green stuff. If things get a little sticky for ol' Tuck, they'll drop him like a snake."

"And so you came here to talk to me about Tuck Loomis and Bernard Island and deeds to lots on the island and all that?"

"I guess I stayed away because I didn't want to talk to you about all that, Wade."

"So let's sit and talk about it, friend. How come you changed your mind about talking to me?"

Wade sat behind his cluttered desk. Brud sat in the chair by the window. "I guess I went through it a little more careful. I've always given you a hard time about how selling real estate and saving the bays and the beaches and the islands are kind of mutually exclusive."

"I thought it was all in fun."

"Well, hell, it was. Maybe here and there in quiet ways you've done more good than I have. Like you blocked that marina thing and got them to locate in a better spot. Anyway, when I found out who was doing the work on Loomis' deeds, I got hold of Rick Riker one day at lunch and pumped him a little. What he said was that Bern had asked him to look the deal over and given him the correspondence, and Rick told Bern that it was a legal arrangement. He told Bern he didn't

33

like the look of it, and he wouldn't get into that sort of thing himself, but he couldn't fault it on any basis within the law."

"So?"

"You're not supposed to sit there and say *So*. You are supposed to say that this whole thing is Bern Gibbs' idea and you fought him on it but he insisted and he went ahead because it's nice money."

"I'll just say that we discussed it and went ahead with it."

"Bern has changed a lot the last few years."

"We all have."

"Look, you're talking to Brud Barnes, your old buddy from way way back. Why the defenses?"

"I'm talking to a newspaper, aren't I? I don't want to read something that says Wade Rowley, half owner of the Rowley/Gibbs real estate agency, said yesterday that he opposed Bernard Gibbs' arrangement with Tucker Loomis for processing the deeds for the Bernard Island Corporation."

"Okay, off the record. Even though I think it would be a good thing if something like that went in the paper. That's true, right?"

"True enough, off the record. And off the record about Bern, he has changed. He's got some kind of inflated image of himself as a hustler. And he's doing a lot of womanizing, and he's spending too much on booze and boats and cars and women. Nita doesn't know anything for sure, but we—Beth and I—think she suspects. And she is one unhappy lady. We had another squabble today about the Bernard Island thing. We get over seventy-five thousand for doing a

34

little bit of clerical work. Tuck doesn't give away money without a reason. He's using us as part of his front, trying to look respectable while he's running a land scam. I don't like it. We may split up over it. And over other things. I don't know yet."

"What I'll maybe do is get back to you one of these days and find out if you want this conversation on the record." He looked at his watch and stood up. "I've got somebody to see."

"Come around oftener. Maybe some fishing?"

"Maybe. Sure." He started toward the door and then turned back to the desk. "This is off the record too. Walk very lightly and carefully, Wade. Look behind every bush. Cover yourself. The F, B and I is taking an interest in this whole thing."

3

On that Monday evening after Wade and Beth Rowley came back from the Bayway Mall with their two children, there was still some daylight left. Tod had studying to do. Kim went next door to play with her best friend. After he had helped her put away the groceries, Wade and Beth went out onto the screened patio behind the house. She turned on the lights in the pool, and began watering some of the patio plantings, complaining about the lack of rain.

He had been staring out into the backyard and he suddenly realized she was standing in front of him, fists on her hips, head tilted.

"I realize you aren't ever real talkative, Mr. Rowley, but this evening you're setting some kind of new record."

"Sorry, honey."

"What is it?"

36

"A long story."

She sat beside him on the couch. "Tell me a story then."

He took her hand and examined it thoughtfully, as if it were a rare and curious object. "Well, I'll tell you a short story first, okay. Then maybe the long one."

"Nice to hear your voice."

"A long long time ago, back when I was still in high school, there was a man about fifty years old here named Conrad Jester. Con was a hustler and he made out pretty well, but he was always on the fringes, never in the big action. He was always looking for the big one and never found it. He was a friend of my dad's. He built some little tract houses, and he bought and sold raw land, and I think he had a little transit mix cement business for a while. Anyway, he got advance news that they were going to build Bay Drive, after talking about it for years. And there was a tract of land there, sixty acres on the west side of town, that was in the Walker family. They had been holding on to it with the idea that someday they could get at least five thousand dollars an acre for it. That is peanuts compared to today's prices. Con Jester struck a deal with them. He would give the Walkers five thousand dollars nonreturnable option money against fifty-six hundred dollars an acre cash money, three hundred and thirty-six thousand. The Walkers wouldn't take any paper. He got to the Walker family a split second before several other parties did. The value of that land once Bay Drive was built was obvious."

"I don't think I'm going to like this story."

"Con Jester had some friends in county government

and city government and they told him he wouldn't have a bit of trouble getting the zoning changed so that he could put up a shopping plaza with plenty of parking. He got hold of an outfit in New Jersey that specialized in planning and leasing shopping centers. Understand, that was almost twenty years ago, so it was early in the game. Their specialists came down and looked the situation over and said they liked the look of it and they would make an arrangement on it favorable to Con. So he took a deep breath and went ahead. He sold everything he owned and came up finally with one hundred and thirty-six thousand dollars. Then he went to the West Bay Citizens Bank and borrowed two hundred thousand at seven percent, with the sixty acres as collateral. Then, of course, all he needed was the zoning change, and he applied for it."

"And they wouldn't give it to him?"

"That's the punch line. He haunted that planning and zoning commission, but he couldn't get anything moving. He began to suspect somebody had set up a roadblock. He called in all his tickets all over town, and he couldn't find out who was blocking him. The interest on his loan came to about twelve hundred a month, which isn't too much these days, but it was enough to eat Con Jester up, because he had sold his income-producing properties to raise the hundred and thirty-six. He'd put down the biggest bet of his life, and they'd closed the table. When he saw what was happening and what probably would happen, he tried to get out of it as best he could. Con was a realist. He made up a little package. At first he tried to get his whole hundred and thirty-six back on a sale to somebody who'd assume the loan. The trouble was there was no alternate use for the land under the zoning they had on it, that would get his bait back. And he couldn't handle that much debt."

"What could he do?"

"If he tried to wait it out, the bank would grab the sixty acres and he'd have nothing left. So he kept dropping the price, spreading the word. And finally when it got down to fifty thousand, a young lawyer—I can't remember his name—showed up and said he represented Pantheon Associates, and he paid the fifty thousand and Pantheon took over the loan and the title.

"A year and a half later, the zoning change was granted and the bulldozers showed up and the sign said that this was the future site of the Bayway Shopping Plaza, a project of Pantheon Associates. The newspaper smoked out the names behind Pantheon a few weeks later. Ellenson, Derks, Loudner, Daggs and the names of a couple of men now long dead. The power structure. The group Tuck Loomis is now a member of. And I guess you could say the group that Con Jester wanted to join."

"How do you know so much about it?"

"As I said, Con Jester and my father were friends. Con died of cancer a few months after the plaza opened. Of course, it's now the Bayway Mall, after the reconstruction a few years back, when they built the professional office building. My father had the theory that the mind and the body are so closely intertwined that if you have some terrible grief or disappointment or public shame, you are more susceptible to cancer and strokes and heart attacks. One Sunday when I went fishing with him, he told me the whole story about Con Jester. It upset him. I guess that's why I remember it so clearly. After he lost that title, Con Jester tried to come back, but his heart wasn't in it. He died almost broke."

Beth straightened up and turned to face him, her eyes shocked and wide. "That's a *terrible* story, Wade."

"Well, let's see. I can change it some. Maybe Conrad Jester, he took that fifty thousand and he did some real smart hustling with it and pumped it up to ten times its size, then met up with that same group again on some kind of deal and really put it to them and came out ahead."

"I don't want to hear fairy stories."

"Well, life has got some bad stories and bad times hung onto it, and the trick is to take your chances at the right time, and hunch back and wait when the time ain't ripe."

"You give me this side meat and grits dialect when you want to settle me down, don't you?"

"Miz Elizabeth, you are a right purty lady. Just a tetch long in the tooth, but holding in there real good. Nice figger of a woman."

"*Lady* is a sexist word. But thanks for the sweet talk. And for the short story. But because of the way Tucker Loomis popped up in the short story, the long story is about him, right?"

"Funny thing, come to think of it. Ol' Tuck came down here from Ohio too, same as you."

"I didn't come down. You brought me down, Mr.

Rowley. But you're kidding about Tucker Loomis, right?"

"Not so. He is as close to the genuine article as you can get, but he did come down twenty-five or so years ago. Friend of his told me once that Tuck scouted the whole coast from Tallahassee to New Orleans, driving a ratty old van, and he finally decided West Bay offered the kind of opportunity he was looking for. So he moved into a downtown motel and put twenty thousand dollars into the Citizens Bank, and a year later he'd married Thelma Casswell, moved into her old family house with her and started building the Gulf Breeze Marina."

"What part of Ohio?"

"I have no idea."

"I hope it wasn't Columbus. I would hate to have it be Columbus. But anyway, you couldn't have been moody this evening on account of something that happened to a man named Mr. Jester a thousand years ago, could you?"

"Pretty and smart, like I always said. Great legs. Great cheekbones. Great brain on her."

So he told her the long story. With interruptions. Kim came home. There was a discussion, not quite an argument, about whether the kids could watch an hour of television violence starting at ten. Tod said that it wasn't fair that he couldn't see what he wanted to see because Kim was too young. It was pointed out to him that it wasn't fair to have all the privileges of his older years, without any exceptions at all. In the end, Tod set the VCR to tape the show so that they could watch it at an earlier hour, and after they had gone to their rooms, Wade and Beth could hear the subterranean thudding of his rock music turned low, like a giant heart beating in a sub-cellar.

When she came out of her bathroom, ready for bed, he put his magazine aside, and hitched over toward the edge of his bed in invitation. She slipped in beside him and he turned the light out.

"That's almost all of it," he said. "Bern was upset. I expected him to be. We've been a good team. We balance each other."

"Didn't he feel at all uneasy about this arrangement?"

"I think so, but he wasn't going to let it show. And he can accept a dog-eat-dog scenario. Here's how Bern would look at that Con Jester situation. He would say that Con could have covered himself if he'd been smart enough. He could have set up the loan on an if-needed basis, paid the Walker family a hundred thousand, with the actual closing and title transfer contingent on a zoning change to what he needed for the shopping plaza. So, in essence, Bern would say Con was punished for being dumb. And the dumb get punished in a lot of ways out there on the streets."

"I have never been really crazy about Bern Gibbs."

"Which you have made abundantly clear to me, but, thank God, not to him."

"Or to Nita. I like her a lot. Bern gives her a real hard time."

"I'm trying to put something into words so that I can understand it a little better. So we both can understand. It isn't easy. The world has changed in an odd way. Back twenty years ago, this town had an actual power structure you could understand. Locally owned banks. The *Daily Press* had local ownership just like the *Courier Journal* still has. We had a fishing fleet and a good-sized boatyard, and some locally owned automobile agencies. The men who owned things and owned big pieces of things, they had clout with city and county government and they served on committees and boards, got the community college started, expanded the hospital, things like that. If you crossed one of them up, you might as well move to Pascagoula because you sure weren't going to amount to much here."

"And now it's different?"

"The banks and the radio stations and Channel Ten and the automobile agencies and most of the larger stores are owned by strangers who live a long way away and who will probably never come to this place. There's a new kind of structure. The developers and local construction firms are the biggest frogs in the pond. But they don't have any kind of continuity. They plan something, sell hell out of it, build it and move to something else. Local government is probably our biggest growth industry, and the good old boys who get themselves settled into local office don't have any check reins on them anymore. They can make their own rules, and the big rule is just don't screw up so bad you can't get elected again. We've got hotshot hustlers who deal in bank paper, tax shelters, penny stocks, commodity straddles, mortgages and things like that. In and out, mostly. Grab and run. What it all is, it's a kind of diffusion. There's no center anymore. There used to be a capital-S Society made up of the

43

wives of the owners of the city enterprises. Now there's a couple or three clubs. That gets me closer to what I want to say.

"Okay, Beth, in this diffusion there's a kind of anarchy. There are no signposts. Tuck Loomis used to do his outside real estate business through Tom French. He still does a little bit of it there. Tom is just a little bigger than we are, but I don't think that on average he's doing as much business as we are. What Tuck Loomis has done is reach out in our direction. I think that either Tom fumbled the ball, or talked back, or forgot lunch, *or* the relationship between Tom French and Tuck Loomis on other deals couldn't stand real close inspection. Tuck has given us a seventy-seven-thousand-dollar warm hug. He has borrowed some of our respectability so that he can use it if he has to when the condemnation suit comes to trial. I can hear him now: 'Your honor, I run all them deeds right through Rowley/Gibbs Associates. Them there are legitimate sales and I got nothing to hide.'"

"What will happen?"

"My guess is he'll opt for a decision by a judge instead of a jury trial, and he'll come into court with big elegant plans and drawings and maps and a tabletop plan of Bernard Island, and a file of sales and mortgages and expensive studies, and the government will win the condemnation suit, but they will have to pay ol' Tuck a very pretty penny, which might work out to five times his investment."

"Then what will happen?"

"If the price is too high, the government will appeal, and they will probably lose and Rowley and

Gibbs will be seventy-seven thousand ahead of where they were before Tuck came along."

"And that's all?"

"Tucker Loomis will be able to ask us for favors whenever he feels like it. He'll be asking Bern. They get along fine. I get along with him, but not as well as Bern. As time goes by I think this business of doing favors and getting favors will turn us into a bigger agency. More money to fix the roof and send the kids to school."

"Then isn't it a good thing?"

"Sort of. Depends on where you stand. Tuck is just a little bit of an outsider, even after twenty-five years. But people who have gone in with him have made money. He plays it very close to the line. So, suppose he gets careless and sloppy and a little bit illegal and is caught. If we are tied in too closely, we could go down with him."

As soon as he said it he felt her sudden tension, the stiffness of her body, and he knew he had made a mistake. Her terrible fear of insecurity was never very far below the surface.

He said quickly, "That's why I'm going to see that we're not tied in that closely. We'll be okay. No pain and no strain." He felt the tension subside as her body relaxed.

She nestled closer in the darkness. "Since when is your big worry the chance you might get caught?"

"I wonder if you know me too well. Wade Rowley, squeaky clean. He finds a quarter in the phone-booth slot, he mails it to the phone company. He thinks good

45

citizens should overpay their taxes. He even goes so far as to—"

"Now hush! All this is serious."

"I know."

"What are you going to do?"

"Well, I have the list of all the thirty-nine people who bought lots way out there on the island. A bunch of them I can cross off. Tuck's pals. Pink Derks, Mr. Daggs, Sam Loudner, Warner Ellenson, Colonel Barkis, Fred Pittman, people like that. And then there's some it would be too much trouble to go looking for because the home addresses are so far from here. One in Miami and one in Portland, Oregon, even. So there's about eleven locals I don't know and I would like to know if they are planning to build out there where the hurricanes blow. Maybe some of them are fronts. Maybe just one."

"And if you find just one?"

"If I find somebody who can't possibly come up with the rest of the money, much less build out there, then I'll try to figure out what the next step should be."

"What's the most drastic thing that could happen, darling?"

"You tell me."

"Sure. Split up with Bern. You told me once if one of you wants out, the other has to buy his stock based on an independent appraisal, and he has ten years to do it. I think most of the people there would want to come with you."

"I wouldn't be too sure of it. The kind of business we are beginning to attract lately, a certain amount of it is from the good old boys. The cute old boys. Bern can solicit and hold that business better than I can. As far as the nuts and bolts of the business are concerned, I know more than Bern. I can work out things when he hasn't got the patience. I know the tax codes better than he does. So if we split up right now and we each took half the business, in ten years he would be big and I would be . . . maybe just about the same."

He heard her sigh. "The roof needs work, maybe replacement. My poor little car goes sour twice a month. Tod isn't going to win any scholarships. Maybe Kim can get one with her tennis. How difficult would it be, being by yourself?"

"Not too bad. Nobody would exactly be steering any business toward me. But it wouldn't be like starting all over."

"Don't get me wrong, darling. But don't you think you could . . . kind of ease off for a while? I mean you could quit looking for problems? I love you because you are exactly the man you are. But this isn't like that terrible story about Mr. Jester. Nobody is actually *stealing* anything. I'll be thirty-six in a week."

"Nobody'd ever know."

"Hush a minute. Look, we can get the kids off to college pretty soon."

"Kim is twelve!"

"You'll be surprised how fast the time will pass. And I can go back to full-time work then instead of this part-time deal. And then there won't be any reason why you can't do what you want to do."

"Honey, I don't *want* to make a fuss. I told Bern that."

"I know. But right now, it just seems so... expensive. You know?"

"I know. That's what I've been thinking about. If I'd been a lot tougher about it when this first came up, then we wouldn't be on the hook the way we are. And Bern wouldn't have fallen in love with the extra money."

She pulled him close and whispered, "This is the first time in maybe a year we've had a long talk about the things that matter most to you."

"I'm right here in bed with what matters most to me."

"I love you so much," she whispered. And he moved his hands along the warm familiar silk of her body, across the beloved places, and heard the catch of her breath in her throat and then her long exhalation.

Later, when he was on the edge of sleep, she said, "I've always liked Helen Yoder. She's had really terrible luck in her life. She seems to do the wrong things at the wrong time. Why would she take up with Tucker Loomis again?"

"For the exercise."

"You're terrible!"

He did not hear her go back to her own bed. He awoke at four and left the bedroom quietly and let himself out onto the patio to stand naked for a time, listening to the tree toads. He stretched out on a chaise, feeling the cool plastic bands against his back and his behind. A mockingbird started up, reestablishing his territory. A slight breeze came out of the southwest and though their home was four blocks from the beach, he could smell the salty, fishy fragrance of the flats. Keep your head down, fella. Do your job. Sell the product, write the contracts, negotiate the loans, attend the closings, bank your share and fatten the Keogh accordingly. Bern is the more cheerful partner. He believes nothing will ever go wrong, really wrong. And you have believed all your life that things can go terribly wrong without warning. Because they did. They proved they could. As someone once said, Life is unfair. Sure. Got the roof fixed just right and along came Hurricane Elena to nudge it out of true and set up the leaks. You can expect a little bit of luck along the way. Beth was proof of that, certainly. And the kids too.

And expect the other kind too. Like when a week before the wedding, his father had taken his wife and Wade's sister out in that old faithful Prowler and anchored at a good spot just off the fastest flow of the outgoing tide. The way they put it together later, after they had caught enough fish and it was time to come home, Ed Rowley had punched the starter button without first running the exhaust fan to clear fumes out of the bilge. Or possibly the exhaust fan did not run properly. So a boat nearby, heading in, saw the orange-red flash, heard the deep whump of explosion, saw chairs and tackle and bodies in the air. Fished the two women out with a boat hook, wrapped them in tarps. Never found the man. Stayed looking until the Prowler burned to the waterline and then went under, hissing and steaming. A shrimp boat found Ed's body two days later. Beth came down with him for the services and stayed, ignoring her family's sharp disapproval. And, in time, when he could lift his head, they were married in a far simpler manner than originally planned.

Over the years the big storms with personal names had taken a lot of lives. As had the diseases of the times. But it was different, somehow, to put your tanned and callused thumb on a silver-shiny button on the instrument panel, press it and get blown away along with the two main women in your life.

And so with the first faint eastern light of the fifteenth day of July, Wade Rowley came upon the memory that had been tucked away so long.

They were over near Pascagoula, Ed Rowley and his son. They had offloaded the dinghy and Ed was poling it through the invisible channels of a mainland tidal marsh. Wade remembered it was a Saturday in the spring. His father was testing him on the names of the marsh plants. Ladies' Tresses, Sweet Bay, Spider Lily, Button Bush, Love Vine, Seedbox, awarding him an imaginary dollar for every one he got right and fining him two for the ones he got wrong. When the breeze died the bugs got too savage, so they poled back to the open water and along the beach to where the Prowler was anchored.

Once they were aboard, Ed lit his pipe and got out three dollars and gave them to Wade. Wade said he thought they'd be imaginary dollars and if he had known they were going to be real, he wouldn't have taken so many chances on the ones he didn't really know. Ed said that all of a sudden he had decided they were real. He said money was a funny commodity. It stood for different things with different people. It could buy almost anything. With some men, he had said, it would buy more than it would with others. It was important, he said, that a man find out early just where he ought to plant his personal For Sale sign. He said that a man who worked for Woodrow Daggs had called him the other day and said Daggs wanted to buy the garage off the Harris property. He would pay for having it moved. He wanted to use it as a construction office on a new job Regal Construction was starting. Ed Rowley had said it wasn't for sale. The man got back to him with double the first offer. Ed said no. When he came back with the offer doubled again, Ed knew he had riled Daggs. A man could build a construction office for half the last offer. He turned it down. He said to Wade, "Boy, it wasn't *what* I was selling. It was *who* I was selling it to. Daggs knew I had no respect for him after the cheap shoddy construction his firm did on the high-school annex. And maybe he knew that when his name came up anywhere, I'd find a way to mention the high-school job. So it wouldn't be I was selling him just the garage. I would be selling him the chance to go around saying that Ed Rowley had helped him out in a time of need when he got caught short needing a construction shack and wasn't that a decent thing for Ed to do? Friends do favors for each other. And it wasn't worth thirty-two hundred dollars for an eight-hundred-dollar garage, to be tied in with a man like Daggs."

And now, Dad, I am tied in with one of them. He too goes around buying approval. Doing favors, and calling them in when he needs them back. He can say,

"Me and Wade Rowley? Sure, we're right close. I run a lot of stuff through Rowley/Gibbs.'"

And you can sit out here in the hour before dawn, boy, and think virtuous thoughts and tell yourself how noble you are and all that shit, and you are going to lay back and hang on to the money, because that is the way the world keeps score. Not your way. Not lately.

4

ade Rowley did not have time to check out the people on his list of eleven names until Wednesday. By early afternoon he had cleared his desk and answered his calls and signed his letters. He called Ellie Service in and had her shut the door and sit across the desk from him. The relationship was good. Ellie was a widow in her late forties. She was a comfortable woman, stocky, self-assured, quiet and quick. She wore rimless glasses, tailored suits and sensible shoes. She wore her gray hair in a smooth Dutch cut with bangs that came down to her thick dark eyebrows. She peered out from under her bangs with a look of skepticism and irony.

He knew that Ellie resented Bern having the larger office even though they were equal partners. Ellie had an intense loyalty. She resented being required to do secretarial work for the sales staff while Bern's secretary, Dawn Marino, worked only for Bern Gibbs. Her resentment was tempered by her understanding of the situation. Bern, with all his service clubs, charity drives, civic memberships and special committees, had a heavier load of outside work. He often took Dawn along to take notes. And Bern probably did not know that the office staff kept track of all the times the two of them returned an hour or so later than was reasonable. Ellie was especially conscious of it because when Dawn was gone, Jeanie Nash, who handled the switchboard and the bookkeeping, patched Bern's calls into Ellie's extension.

"How are things out there?" he asked.

"Ah yes. Out there on the floor. We have a demonstration of one of the first rules of galley slaving. If you put all the rowers on one side of the boat, it goes in a circle."

"Who this time?"

"Mr. Mettler. He's making up this promotional thing. He has a new little Sony camera . . ."

"He showed it to me. It makes tapes he can play on his VCR."

"So he's making a tape movie of the office, of all the people. He pans on you, whatever that is, and you have to smile and look sincere and then he does this 'voice over,' which means that he speaks very loud and slow and says, 'And this is Miss Joyce Kindred, one of our most valuable salespersons. Joyce has been with us now for umpty years and she specializes in residential properties and condominiums.' As I understand it, he will take a tape player with a little television screen on it and carry it about and play it for anybody who will

54

watch it. It will improve our image. I think he wants to write off his equipment. What he does, he erases everybody about nine times before he gets an interview he likes."

Frank Mettler was an enigma, a round brown bouncy man with a shaven skull and huge black eyebrows. Each time they had almost decided to start easing Frank out, he would perform some extraordinary service. And he had enlisted a cadre of housewives, widows and divorced women to work part-time for the agency. He had trained them, tutored them so they could pass the required examinations, and gave out little gilt stars for good work. They adored him and worked hard for him. He had turned pointless lifestyles into energy and money. Those who failed to adore him were eased out, quite gently.

He involved himself in general office administration, advertising and promotion, recruiter and coordinator of the part-time salespeople, and sometime salesperson himself. Wade knew he did not want to go and talk to Frank. Frank always stood too close to whomever he was honking at, grinning and twitching and shuffling his feet. He did not want to ask Frank why he was making a home movie of the office. He did not want to listen to the answers, all fifty-three of them. Maybe this project would not turn out to be an iron balloon, as did so many of his ideas. Maybe this one would fly. Maybe his growing platoon of parttimers adored being taped.

"I'll wait and see," he said.

"I thought you'd say that. Otherwise all is well out there. I mean as well as usual."

"How's your good friend at the Credit Bureau."

"Kitty has a new friend. He's teaching her to sail. She goes about in a constant condition of sunburn and the squints."

"Could you get her to do a fast confidential survey of these eleven names? Very simple question. Would it be okay to sell each of them a building lot for a hundred and fifty thousand dollars, with a very small down payment and an adjustable rate mortgage?"

Ellie read the names. "No formal report?"

"Verbal is good enough. Maybe not over the office phones, hers or ours."

"I can give her the list tonight and get it back Thursday night. Is that soon enough?"

It pleased him that she did not ask why things had to be kept confidential. She knew he would tell her in good time.

"That will be fine. Is Helen out there?"

"She's probably still there. Send her in?"

Helen Yoder came striding in, smiling, and he waved her into the chair. She wore a baggy blouse of coarse white cotton with a blue stripe, and a narrow skirt.

"Very nice work on that Crown property," he said. "When's the closing?"

"September first. A Monday. Two in the afternoon at Citizens instead of the title company. The estate is in their trust department. It will be a clean deal. The estate will take back a first mortgage, no points charged."

"How is the marina deal coming along?"

"Dead, maybe. His father backed out. Not exactly

backed out, but finally told Andy he was lying about having that much money. I don't think Bruce has the credit rating to swing it."

"So what are you working on?"

"Some junk. I'm trying to find a house for a woman who hasn't liked anything yet. Not ever. Not ever in her whole life. And I'm trying to talk somebody into giving us an exclusive on some raw land mostly on account of I have a friend in a law firm that's splitting up and they are thinking of putting up a building and selling it and leasing it back. Other than that, nothing. Resting on my laurels. And straightening out my files. Once they're in order, I want to ask Jeanie to put them on the hard disk. Is that okay?"

"Sure."

"She's been teaching me how to access stuff. Maybe I ought to get my own compatible, like Bruce has. Then I could tap into the multiple listings and get a fresh list every time, without the junk that's been sold or withdrawn and not taken off. I could take a course."

He was aware of her unusual vitality. Whenever she came in, she made his small office seem smaller. There was so much animation, such an almost palpable throbbing of life force.

"Was there something in particular you wanted?" she asked.

"I guess not. I was going to ask your advice about something, but I've decided it's an imposition."

"Wade, my advice about anything isn't worth much, but feel free to ask."

He searched his mind for a reasonable question and

could not find one. "No. I'll give it some more thought and maybe get back to you later."

As she left his office she turned and gave him a puzzled look. He could not blame her. It had been a dumb performance. He had planned to try to get her talking about Tuck Loomis, but had been unable to think of any way to get it started. He wanted to hear that Tuck was a fine fellow, honest as the day is long. But he knew he would never hear that. There would be a wink, a nudge, a sly whisper. "They don't put much over on ol' Tuck." But that didn't mean he was dishonest, did it? He was shrewd. No law against that.

On Friday, July eighteenth, a hundred and fifty miles from West Bay, the foursome teed off on the number-two course at Longleaf at two-thirty. It was a blinding hot day, the air thick as smoke, the fairways baked to fuzzy concrete. The canopies on the electric carts were essential. Usually Judge D. Henry Swane of the U.S. District Court was paired with Stu Persons, the builder, and Billy DeVine, the Mercedes dealer, was paired with Doc Crocker, the neurologist. But in mid-morning Stu Persons had phoned the Judge and said he couldn't make their Friday game and he was sending out a fellow to take his place, a fellow named Dennis Short from West Bay, in the construction business, a nice guy, claiming a handicap of twelve, same as Stu Persons.

The three regulars watched the newcomer narrowly as he took his practice swings on the first tee. He was younger than the rest of them, a thin chap with big hands, a knit shirt, pink slacks and a golf hat with AU-

GUSTA NATIONAL embroidered on it. His was a controlled swing, slow and easy, with a brisk clack of clubface on ball, a carry of over a hundred and sixty yards and a bounding rollout past two hundred. Down the middle.

Billy and Doc and the Judge felt irritable. Their regular session was a lot of fun. They enjoyed the press bets and the most that ever changed hands was six or seven dollars. This young fellow seemed to be out of their class. He rode along with the Judge in Stu Persons' cart, and the Judge drove. Dennis Short pushed his iron off to the right beyond the trap into some scrub, scuffed his approach and took three putts for a six. The Judge had a five, and Billy and Doc had a four and a seven. So the teams split the hole, and Billy took low ball, and they felt better about the stranger among them. He was affable and polite, expressing admiration of a good shot and sympathy for a bad one. He didn't stand in anyone's way, and he didn't fiddle about aimlessly or talk when he shouldn't. And best of all, he didn't play as well as they had at first feared.

The long lack of rain, very unusual for this time of year, helped the Judge's game. He always hit low balls down the middle, and used pitch and run on his approaches. In marshy conditions, he picked up too many double bogeys. On these baked lands he got an incredible roll, and had to be wary of rolling over the greens. He was playing far better than his handicap of fifteen, and it cheered him.

They were able to move along briskly until they made the clubhouse turn and came up on slower players at the eleventh hole. The Judge pulled over into the shade of a big yellow pine at the right side of the fairway. Doc and Billy were over in the far rough, waiting. The foursome ahead had just begun to putt out.

"When he heard I was coming over here, Warner Ellenson said to say hello if I happened to run into you, Judge."

Judge Henry Swane turned his head quite slowly and studied the man sitting beside him, as if seeing him for the first time.

"And how is Warner these days?"

"Very well. I'll tell him you asked about him. He said to tell you he's been following a little Colorado company called Maxim engineering listed on the National. They've done some interesting work on cellular telephone techniques. It goes for about nine dollars a share. He thinks there's going to be a fat buyout."

"Warner has a lot of luck in the market."

The green was clear. The Judge hit first, scuffed the ball slightly, but got a roll which took it right to the edge of the green.

"Very nice!" Dennis Short said, and addressed the ball with a six iron, lofted it high and far, a soft shot that landed like feathers and curled on back toward the cup.

"A lot nicer!" said the Judge.

"A little luck here and there," said Dennis Short.

When, even though there was ample opportunity to chat, Dennis Short made no further mention of Warner Ellenson, Judge Swane knew it was up to him to raise the subject. He found himself admiring Short's tact and reserve.

On the long fourteenth when they were waiting while Billy and Doc looked for Doc's slice in the right rough, the Judge said, "What's Warner doing lately?"

"This and that. You know how he is. He's been into a situation with the man I work for. Woody Daggs, Regal Construction. They each bought a couple of lots on Bernard Island. A man named Tucker Loomis was developing the island, and all of a sudden the Park Service came along and grabbed it for a very low dollar. Woody and Warner think Mr. Loomis is being jerked around."

"What does this Loomis think?"

"He thinks the Park Service will have to come up with a lot more money after it's heard in court. He's told my boss that he thinks the U.S. Attorney will have a very weak case. That's why he wants a nonjury trial. Of course, nobody can build on the island now. My boss was going to put up a super-deluxe lodge out there behind the dunes. Too bad. But I guess the government has to stop the development of the barrier islands. Look what the last couple of hurricanes did out there."

"They found it. Billy's about to hit. He's off his game today."

"Very nice guy. Both of them. Fun to play with."

As they drove toward the Judge's ball, he said, "I need this kind of relaxation. I never play with lawyers and I never play with anybody who has a pending action that might be in my courtroom."

"That's very wise, Judge. A man in your position can't afford to take chances."

"There are always people looking for any opportunity to snipe at you," said the Judge. He decided to try a wood off the fairway. He was two hundred yards from the green, and a few feet from the left rough. He took his three wood. As he waggled, he gave himself messages. Knees slightly bent, right hand far enough over, keep the head steady, turn the hips first, slight pause at the top, swing at it—don't scoop it. On the downswing he realized he had given himself too many orders, confusing the body, locking up the swing. He lunged and hit it off the heel of the club. Not enough toward the heel to create a darter that would bolt into the shrubbery, but enough to slam the ball left at a low sizzling angle, whipping the tops of tall grasses, chunking a thick tree about two feet from ground level, hitting it at a slight angle which corrected the flight of the ball and sent it toward the green. It rolled swiftly through a shallow trap and the far lip of the trap sent it high in the air. It fell onto the green and rolled dead about five feet from the cup. He realized that had he hit it squarely, he would have been fifty yards over the green.

He beamed at Dennis Short. "You can be good, or you can be lucky," he said. "Me, I'll take lucky."

At a little after four on Sunday afternoon, Tucker Loomis got up from his nap on the maroon leather couch in his study, took a bottle of dark Pauli Girl out of his office refrigerator, uncapped it, took several swallows and then strolled through the long living room to the bedroom wing and down to the last bedroom on the right, the one that looked out over the flower gardens.

Maria, the nurse on duty, was watching television, the volume turned low. She saw him out of the corner of her eye, and sprang to her feet, smiling. Of the three private nurses, she was the only one who wore the traditional white, cap and all. The other two, and the spare who filled in, all came to work looking like ball girls at a tennis tournament. But they were good. All of them.

He winked at Maria and went over to the hospital bed. The head and the knees were cranked up. Thelma Casswell Loomis wore a quilted pink bed jacket and she had a pink ribbon fastened to her sparse white curls. It was the second stroke a year ago which had done most of the damage, paralyzing her right side and killing the language and comprehension centers in the left brain. The right side of her face sagged, distorting the eye and the mouth.

He pulled the chair close to the side of the bed and took her left hand. When he squeezed it, it squeezed back. She always looked at him with a strange earnest expression in her eyes, and tried to talk to him, but made strange sounds. "Gaa nah gaan." Limited sounds, the *ah* sound plus the hard *g* and the *n*."

"Hey, Mother," he said. "I talked to both boys this morning and I came in to tell you and you were having a nap. Everything is fine with the boys, and their ladies, and our grandkids. I talked to everybody. They all send their love. Cass told me Kathie is pregnant again, and when she has the third, they'll be two up on Brent and Jessie."

He talked on, holding her hand, talking into that anxious and earnest and appealing expression, knowing full well she understood not one word of it. She could understand gestures of command—turn the head, squeeze the hand, raise the foot, close the eyes. But those same commands, spoken, meant nothing to her. Her anxiety was an anxiety to communicate. He really could not tell whether it helped or hurt to keep coming in and talking to her—whether it made it better or worse—but it seemed to be the only thing to do. At least it made him feel as if he were part of a family. He wished the kids were closer. It might ease the burden some. But the little ones wouldn't understand at all. He told her all the news he could remember.

Sometimes in the middle of the night he would think about her in the nearby bedroom and wonder how it would be if you could not label the things that happened in your head. If you were cold, you would have no word for it, only a sensation you could not name. There would be no words for lonely, hungry, fear, pain, sorrow, hate, nausea, politics, money or Chicago. Words triggered concepts. It must be a strange place inside her head, with blurred and drifting *things* that had no names.

He leaned and kissed her forehead, released her hand and stood up. "Well, Mother, I'm going to wander on down to Warner's place because this time of day he'll be wallowing around in the pool with that nutty dog of his, and we've got a little bit of business to take care of. You be good now, hear?"

Maria followed him out into the hall. "How's it going, chica?" he asked.

"Okay. I think she likes the ribbon. I held the mirror and she reached up and touched it and the left side of her mouth went up, which is as close as she can come to smiling. Okay, she had her massage and she ate all the soup and Jell-O and she had a good bowel movement."

"How bored are you?"

"Me? I don't know. What the hell. I'm off at four. I read and I watch the television, and I watch those cassettes."

"So far three nurses quit on me. I don't want to lose you."

"Look, you keep paying, there's a lot of us out there. It doesn't matter if somebody quits, right?"

"I'd hate to lose the prettiest one."

"Some kind of talk."

He edged her back against the wall, put his hand on her waist. He smiled into her eyes and saw how they changed.

"I don't want we should be doing this," she said uncertainly.

"So this isn't the right time anyway, sweet girl," he said in a guttural whisper. "Tomorrow Henry doesn't come work on the yard and Lottie doesn't show up until noon. So what you do, hear, after you relieve Mrs. Hardigan and you go in and pat Thelma's pillow, you come in and you surprise me awake. Can you do that?"

She looked sidelong at him and bit her lip. Her eyes were very dark, her skin flawless. There was a glint of mischief in her eyes. "I guess if you want to be waked up, well . . . that's kind of what a nurse does, isn't it?"

"Surely is, and I'll be right grateful to you."

He walked out of the house feeling tired of himself,

depressed by the recurring insistence of the groin, the slow engorgements, the fantasies. He had known that sooner or later, if she kept working, he would get to her. He had known he was making progress, that she was no longer thinking of him as an old white-haired fellow who liked to flirt with her, that she had begun to wonder what it would be like if it happened. He was a little surprised it would happen so soon. He had guessed it would take another week or two. His pleasurable anticipation of her body was diminished by his vague sense of disappointment. He had wanted it to take longer. He had wanted it to be more difficult to arrange. So it would happen and happen again in sweet abundance, until predictably Maria would fade back into the endless swamps of his memories of women, any uniqueness of breasts or buttocks or lovesounds lost in the general turmoil of sweating and pumping and coming.

And doing it to another one in the house where Thelma lay helpless would add another mild increment of guilt. She'd been asleep when she had the second stroke. She was exhausted. They had stayed up very late, quarreling over his having taken the Rigsby woman to New Orleans. How the hell was anybody to know they'd run head on into that damned Morrison bitch who would run, not walk, to the phone to tell Thelma. A long and bitter and noisy quarrel, with her saying that because she'd had the stroke which slurred her speech and gave her the little limp, she was no longer attractive to him. There had been other quarrels across the years, about other women, but this had been the worst. She had not said good night, and, of course, had never been able to say good night or anything else from then on.

Warner Ellenson was in the big screened pool with Albert, the golden retriever, throwing Albert's floating yellow bone for him to retrieve, wallowing and splashing around and barking at each other.

Ellenson was a big, overweight man, soft and pink and rubbery, and in far better condition than he looked. He swam fifty laps a day, walked six miles, and kept a pink thumb in lots of pies. As an ex-mayor, he had the use of a tiny office in the court house, and what stenographic help he could wheedle. He was a class-A wheedler. He had been known to pick up a lunch check, but nobody could remember exactly when or where.

He clambered out of the pool in his absurd little bikini shorts and went dripping to the outdoor bar and fixed the two of them bourbon on the rocks, a generous measure, but cheap bourbon.

They sat at a tin table in the shade. The dog bobbed about in the pool looking imploringly at his master, yellow bone in his jaws, barking "Marph, marph!" He gave up, climbed the steps out of the pool, shook himself so vigorously in the sunshine that Tuck could see little rainbows in the spray, then came over to Warner and dropped the bone at his feet. When Warner ignored it, the dog sighed and collapsed under the table in the shade, and was instantly asleep.

"How's Thelma doing?" Warner asked.

"Same as ever. No change. And there won't be any. But thanks for asking. How did it work out?"

"Just fine. Woody's old pal, this Stu Persons, was very obliging about it. He arranged to have Dennis take his place in the foursome."

"That there Dennis Short has a lot of promise. Woody's got hisself a real good boy there."

"It went just the way we thought it would. And it put D. Henry Swane in the side pocket again. He was sure a big help to me when I had my troubles. But in this case it seems kind of like overkill."

"Why be safe when you can be double safe? What I was afraid of, if the federal case is a legitimate case but the presentation is too damned weak, too obviously weak, my lawyer buddies tell me a judge can declare a recess and tell the government to go do some home- work and come back better prepared. It hasn't hap- pened often, but it *has* happened. I want that Swane to sit quiet, and I want him to buy my figures. I don't want any kind of compromise arithmetic going on."

"Speaking of arithmetic, I think the Judge is going to be a very happy man in a couple of weeks. Sure you don't want to pick up some of that Maxim Engineer- ing?"

"Now wouldn't that be smart?"

"You're right. It would be dumb. Woody and me and the Colonel, we've been picking it up right along at six and seven and eight dollars. Little nibbles be- cause the sucker is real thin. Anyway, Woody arranged to have some tout sheets mailed off to the Judge's home address. And he's smart enough to save them to show why he got interested, in case it ever comes up."

"I've been having too much on my mind to fool with the market lately. I cashed my chips and dumped it into tax-free money market. I've got to keep a close eye on this suit."

"What happens next?"

"My people keep working their ass off on the presentation, and we wait for a date for the proceedings."

"You want to know something funny?"

"What?"

"I mean it's weird, Tuck. Ever since I bought that land and then the architect showed me the rendering of how my place would look, I've been thinking about a place like that out on that island, a real private place. When I'm going to sleep I walk through the rooms and figure out where things go, and what the windows will look out at. I see the birds out there. I mean I got to believe in it so much, it was like a loss to me, a personal loss, when the Park Service grabbed it and stopped it from happening."

"Just keep on feeling that way, Warner."

"But only a pure damned fool would put heavy money into anything out on those islands."

"I didn't hear that."

"You serious?"

"Believe me, I was going to build the showplace of the whole Gulf of Mexico. For the big rich. Private lives. Security, luxury. In the kitchen of the club there'd be a world-famous chef. That island was going to be like a cruise ship parked out there, lights shining at night. Waves rolling on the beach. Music. I was going to have structures hurricanes couldn't touch. Million-dollar houses, Warner. There was going to be fifty beautiful one-million-dollar houses and a ten-million-dollar club."

"You feeling all right?"

"I feel just fine, Warner. But I feel cheated. They took my dream away from me."

"I wasn't going to put any million dollars into my house."

"You'd probably want to park a mobile home out there."

"I thought of doing that. Sure. Until I could figure out just how to place the main house."

"See you around, Warner. Thanks for the drink. And thanks for the progress report."

"Always glad to oblige."

And that was good old Warner, he thought as he walked home. Always glad to oblige, if it didn't cost him anything. A thud and rumble of thunder startled him. He stopped and turned and saw the tall thunderheads in the southwest, twin forks of pink lightning stabbing down just as the sun began to disappear behind the edge of the tallest storm. By now Warner's dog would be under Warner's bed, shuddering and whimpering, and Warner would be there soothing him.

Maria was gone. And when he tried to remember the name of the one who always came on at four, there was a blank spot in his brain where the name should have been. Thelma was sleeping again, and the motorized bed had been cranked down to flatness. There was a small lamp with a pink shade on the night table. The draperies were pulled across the windows. He could hear the rain beginning, the big drops first, and he heard the thunder move closer.

He remembered he had told the housekeeper he

would eat down at the club but he could not remember if he had made a date with anyone. It was too early to go down there. If he went now, he would drink too much.

He went into the closet in his study, turned on the light and worked the combination on the barrel safe in the closet wall. He took out a small package and placed it on his desk blotter. The tiny ivory carving was wrapped in a square of soft dark red cloth. It was a *netsuke* of the eighteenth century, carved by Masanao of Kyoto, a toggle once used by the Japanese to hold the partitioned box which contained personal possessions, the cord between box and toggle threaded behind the sash.

He examined it through a glass. It was a seated rat, tail curled around its body, scratching its ear with one hind paw. The large eyes were inlaid. It was signed on the belly in an oval reserve. The toned ivory had minute age cracks, one of them crossing the right eye. It was a splendid piece by one of the great masters. His London agent had bid it in at Sotheby's for twelve thousand pounds, over eighteen thousand dollars with the buyer's premium on the hammer price.

He stroked the elegance of the ivory with the tip of his finger, and he had the feeling the glossy eyes were looking at him. One day, he thought, I will have the finest collection of Masanao *netsuke* in the world. The Loomis collection. And I will give it to one of the great museums of art. Already he owned ten superb pieces.

He folded the ivory rat carefully into the cloth, put it in the safe and spun the dial. Because the rain was still coming down after he had changed, he drove down to the club.

"Hey, there he is!" the guys yelled. "Hey, Tuck! Over here! What kept you?"

And he smiled to think that if he told them what had kept him, they would begin to believe he was losing his wits.

5

Wade Rowley finally found the Feeney place in the late afternoon on Wednesday, the twenty-third of July. It was west of the city beyond the solid waste dump which drained toxic wastes down into the broad salt marsh, and was the object of endless meetings, resolutions and demands, none of which changed the fact that there was no other sanitary landfill site available at the present time.

The dirt road turned right off Lamarr, and the heavy rains of Sunday night and Monday had scoured the dust and left puddles in the ruts. In the heat of late afternoon he could smell the murky acid of the dump and hear the bulldozers grunting and shoving.

There was a mailbox out by the end of the driveway, shaded by an old live oak, with FEENEY printed on it in crooked capitals. The narrow lot was deep, and the travel trailer was parked toward the back of the lot, between two live oaks bigger than the one out by the road.

Wade parked his blue Ford in the shade near the trailer, turned the engine off and got out. He heard a shrilling of insects, a mockingbird in the oak tree and an intermittent rumbling sound which he finally identified as a dog growl. It was a big mottled dog with a broad head and a deep chest. It was in a wire run next to the trailer, sitting like a library lion, pale yellow eyes watching him as it growled. He started to go toward the trailer to knock on the door, but the dog stood up and increased the volume, pulling his lips back in a snarl. The chicken wire looked flimsy. Wade went back to the car, opened the door and blew the horn.

Nobody appeared. The dog sat again. In the mild breeze from the north, Wade cold hear distant truck traffic on Interstate 10. He looked at his watch and decided he would give this Feeney twenty minutes. He sat behind the wheel and read an office copy of the contract between the Bernard Island Corporation and Ezra Feeney. Boob Davis had signed for the corporation as secretary and treasurer, and someone had penciled the book number and page number of the recording of the deed on the top right corner of the first page. For a mortgage deed it had some special exceptions Wade had never seen before. Of course now it was scrap paper. The federal government owned the land the deed was intended to transfer. Feeney's signature looked carefully drawn, the tongue-in-the-corner-of-the-mouth calligraphy of the unlettered. The contract acknowledged the receipt of five thousand dollars against a price of ninety-five thousand dollars for lot number 106.

Just as he reached for the ignition key an old white pickup truck drove in. It swung around and parked ahead of him. The tires were bald and it was rusted out. A lean stooped man got out. He had a long face, thin red hair going gray. He wore neatly pressed dark blue trousers and a white shirt. He wore a dark pistol belt with a buttoned holster.

"Mr. Feeney, I'm Wade Rowley and I—"

"Hold it a minute," the man said. He went and unlatched the wire door to the dog run and held it open. The big dog trotted off into the empty lot next door, into the tall brush.

The man shook his head. "I tried to make it big enough, he could empty hisself in some corner of it, but the damned fool, he won't go where he lives. Has to hold it all day until I get home, and that can't be easy because he ain't a young dog anymore. His name is Fred. He's one good old dog. Who'd you say you are?"

"Wade Rowley. I wanted to ask you a couple of questions about this deed to the land you bought on Bernard Island."

"I guess I'm not going to get that land after all. That's what they say. You like a cold beer?"

"I sure would."

"Let me get Fred his supper first."

They sat at a bench beside a table next to the trailer and drank out of the bottles. Ezra Feeney looked at the deed and handed it back. "That's it," he said. "What is there to ask about? Over, isn't it?"

75

"That's hard to say for sure, Mr. Feeney. Let's say you had a certain amount of disappointment in not getting to buy the land. Mental anguish maybe. So when the government pays up, maybe they ought to pay for that too."

"Well, that would be a nice thing, wouldn't it? But shit, man, I never could have bought that land. Mr. Tuck knew it and I knew it. He said he'd give me time on it, but he could have give me three ordinary life-times and I couldn't have kept up with the interest. He said I was to be real sincere about buying it and own-ing it, and I was, until all of a sudden the government took it over."

"I keep thinking I've seen you before."

"I used to live here in West Bay. I came back maybe a year ago. I was gone from here ever since I was sev-enteen. My daddy used to work at Foley's boatyard, that's now Gulf Breeze Marina. When they launched the biggest boat they ever built in that yard, it was just thirty years ago this past spring, they waited on a high tide to slide it on down the ways. You come from here?"

"Yes, I do."

"Then maybe you heard of it, heard somebody talk about it. It got jammed on one of the blocks and my daddy ran to sledge it out of there and he'd been drinking to celebrate and he tripped and fell forward and that big old boat it plain mashed him flat on the way down. He screamed one time. I heard that. Over all the other noise, I heard that. I was there learning the business. And I left that same week and never came back until I guess it was a year ago. I never had anything to do with building boats, not again in my life, not since then."

"I did hear about it. That must have been a terrible thing."

Ezra Feeney finished his bottle of beer. "It was a long time ago. And I've been so many places, you know, I can't remember much what he looked like. His name was Fred. Every dog I've ever had, I named him Fred. What'd you want to ask me?"

"What kind of work do you do? Bank guard?"

"Hell no. I don't think I could come up with the references to get a job like that. I'm a gate guard up at Parklands, Mr. Tuck's place out there on the river. For a while, anyway. I get itchy and then me and Fred, we move along. Never have no trouble finding something to do. You just keep asking until you get something."

"Well, what do you think your mental anguish is worth, being deprived of the land you wanted to buy and build on?"

"You kidding me?"

"Name a figure."

"Oh, I'd say in the neighborhood of ten thousand. And that's a nice neighborhood." He laughed and hit himself on the thigh.

"You were just pretending to be a buyer?"

Feeney looked at him, lips pursed. "If you're working on this for Mr. Tuck, then you know what the deal was. And if you're not, what are you trying to do? You wouldn't be government, would you?"

"I'm half of Rowley/Gibbs real estate. This contract was printed in our offices."

"I've seen your signs around. Okay. I have to watch

myself. I talk too much. Always have. Always will. My tongue gets out ahead of my thinking."

"I guess I saw you at Parklands, on the gate. We don't live there but I get out there now and then. I guess I was about eight years old when you left town. I remember everybody talking about the man who got killed at the launching."

"It was the biggest boat ever built there. There were lots of people around. It was all over the paper next morning."

Wade stood up. "Thanks for your help."

"Where do I go for my ten thousand?" the man asked, grinning. His teeth were in sorry shape.

"Somebody will tell you. I've got a list of names of other people I have to contact, with the addresses. You know any of them?"

He handed the typed list to Ezra Feeney. "Just this here one, Jack Simms. He's a drinking buddy of mine. He's the dockmaster out at Parklands. He's got alimony eating him up. He couldn't buy land any more than old Fred dog here can. Or me either."

Wade Rowley met with Gordon Hammond at two o'clock on Sunday afternoon in the lobby of the Holiday Inn on Route 49 about ten minutes from the Gulfport Municipal Airport.

Wade recognized the man from having met him at a public hearing in West Bay when the Barrier Island National Seashore concept was being discussed. Hammond was a rangy rawboned graying man in a khaki business suit and blue running shoes. He had the tan of a life spent out of doors, shaggy gray eyebrows, deep lines across his forehead and bracketing his mouth, and a nose askew from an old break.

"Rowley?" Hammond said, peering at him with intense interest. "You were the one kept bringing up the salt marsh pollution problem. I asked about you. Didn't sound to me like a real estate salesman."

"The better the environment, the easier it is to sell the very best property. I appreciate your flying down."

"Pretty mysterious phone call."

They went into the coffee shop, to a corner booth. Hammond listened without comment or change of expression as Wade Rowley told him of his agency's connection with Tucker Loomis and the Bernard Island Corporation. He told him of the thirty-nine mortgage deeds they had processed before the Park Service had shut Loomis down by taking over the island and putting the seven hundred thousand dollars aside for the purchase.

"Here, Mr. Hammond, are copies of our office copies of four of the deeds we processed and recorded. I've talked to just one of the buyers, Mr. Ezra Feeney. He admits that he would be unable to buy land that expensive. I made a confidential credit check on these other three, Simms, Stanfield and Phipps, and they are in the same position. All four of them work for Tucker Loomis. So these agreements to buy land are essentially fraudulent."

Gordon Hammond sighed audibly and stared down into his coffee as he stirred it. "Let me go into a little bit of history, Wade. When we picked up the islands, Horn, East and West Ship and Petit Bois, for the Gulf Islands National Seashore, it was a very good move.

79

Those islands create a low-salinity, high-nutrition habitat for coastal marine life in Mississippi Sound. We should have picked up Bernard Island at the same time. But we didn't. And now we will."

"But it is going—"

"To be more expensive? You bet. The government moves like a huge blob of molasses on a two-degree slope. Everything gets done two years from next Tuesday. Everything we in the Park Service want to do is previewed by committees of the House and the Senate. Always, always, always there are leaks. The word gets out. And there is always some smartass little dipstick hustler jumping in and getting title and making big plans, hoping to screw his government out of some money. We are fair game for the Tucker Loomises of this society. So this is just one more example of how things work. It's the Tucker Loomises who get those committee members elected again and again, so when something comes along worth knowing, who do you think they are going to tell?"

"I didn't mean to inconvenience you for—"

"There are safeguards, of course. The U.S. Attorney will be able to show the Court that the idea of a residential development on a transient island ten and a half miles off shore is absurd on the face of it. The man would never be able to get the permissions. So suppose the Court gives the developer an award we think too high. There is always the process of appeal. And, at any time, there is always the process of friendly negotiation possible. But I'll hang onto these, Wade, and make sure the U.S. Attorney's Office gets them. After they're presented in evidence, the judge might have some interesting questions for Mr. Loomis."

"I feel as if I've wasted your time, Mr. Hammond."

"Please call me Gordon. I'm getting too damned close to retirement as it is. Mr. Hammond makes me feel decrepit. And you haven't wasted my time. This Loomis fellow is a little more brash than most. I'll add a letter to the file we've sent to the U.S. Attorney. The more one project costs us, the less we have for the next. And things are getting tighter and tighter up there. You know the Pascagoula Swamp well?"

"I went up the river into the swamp maybe a dozen times with my dad, back in the sixties."

"People down here do not know—most of them— just how lucky they are. That weird combination of Graham Wisner and the Pascagoula Hardwood Company and Dan Morine of The Nature Conservancy, along with Avery Wood of the Mississippi Game and Fish Department, they prodded the state into setting up the Mississippi Wildlife Heritage Committee. So what you have in the Pascagoula is a thirty-two-thousand-acre piece that cleanses the water coming down the river and nourishes it as it goes into the Sound."

Wade Rowley kept an attentive look on his face as Gordon Hammond gave him an overview of the geological uniqueness of Mississippi Sound. His father had talked about it a hundred times on their boating and camping and hunting trips. His father had had little education, but he'd read everything he could find about the flora and the fauna and the structure of this place where he had grown up. And having read of something, he had to go out and try to find it and look at it. Together they had been on each of the islands. On Ship, before Camille turned it into East Ship and West Ship. On Dauphin, Deer, Round, Cat, Bernard, Horn, Petit Bois, the Chandeleur Islands. His father had made him realize what a fantastic long-lasting event had begun to take place fifteen thousand years ago when the meltwaters of the receding glaciers had come streaming and hissing and roaring down off the low hills to the north, gouging out the river valleys, shoving soil and rock and sand and gravel and mud out into the north Gulf where it settled and where the wave and tide action had formed the barrier islands twelve miles offshore. On maps his father had showed him how the great curve of the Chandeleurs was the result of the deposit of all that alluvium, the scrapings of a continent, and how the great bays, Mobile, Biloxi and St. Louis, had been formed by this unleashed energy.

He knew the things Hammond was telling him, how the great swamps and wetlands nourished the Sound and the northern Gulf. He remembered his father picking up a few dead leaves, tupelo and gum. "Look like nothing, these leaves. You take a hundred pounds of them, boy, they float down the river and where the river spreads out into swamp, they sink and they rot, and you know what? That hundred pounds will set free about eight pounds of protein to float on downstream. Food for the fish critters. Old rotten logs, green algae, moss, plankton, all doing the same thing. You remember that."

The freshwater swamps and the saltwater marshes had their chores to perform in the life cycles of plants and animals. And his father knew the plants of the marshlands—Bed Straw and Ox Eye, Seedbox and Frog Fruit, Strangleweed and Dropwort—and he knew the creatures of the Gulf waters—blue crabs, grass shrimp, hermits, coquinas, sea anemones and sea leeches. "Use your eyes, boy! Use your brain. Every living thing works together with other living things. Figure out how."

And now Hammond was talking about places along the coast which had gone bad. About the Biloxi Tchoutacabouffa River system where raw sewage was entering the river from over a hundred different points, and the downriver stench was memorable. About the quarter ton of sewage sludge pumped into Ocean Springs Harbor every day because the sewage plant was inadequate for the population growth. About the salt marshes along the coast being filled and being used in many cases as garbage dumps. And Wade's father had been dead sixteen years. Wade thought once again how he would have hated what was happening. And no way to stop it, apparently.

He suddenly realized Hammond was talking about something he had not heard before and he brought his attention into focus. "... over there on the Alabama border, there is a relatively new chemical landfill dump with a lot of highly toxic shit going into it, and we've recently learned that the water-table flow is in the direction of the Pascagoula. Wade, it is a very narrow margin of safety for the Sound if nothing harms the Pascagoula and if the barrier islands remain wild. But, if the Pascagoula starts to die, then in a very short time this whole Sound will start to die and there won't be one goddamn thing anybody can do to stop it. No plants, no animals, *nothing!*" And as he said the final word he slammed his fist on the table, startling the few other customers in the coffee shop and spilling coffee.

"Sorry. I get too worked up," Hammond said. He smiled. "By now I ought to be able to take the long view. But you feel helpless. We're in an endless war with the developers, a very critical and deadly war, and they don't even know they're in one. All they know is that if they are patient enough and generous enough and amiable enough, sooner or later they can pry some more fragile marshland from the politicians and take it away from the people forever. They rip it out of the ecosystem so completely it is as if it never existed. They put up condominiums and increase the sewage load, the traffic load, fire and police protection, water supply, education costs. But they make enough to join the right clubs, drive the right cars and build their own homes overlooking the water. And they go to breakfast work sessions of the Chamber of Commerce and the Committee of One Hundred to talk about the problems of the future of the Gulf area. And after they are dead, the damage they do goes on and on, visited on their descendants forevermore. Their great-grandchildren will live in a world that is drab, dirty, ugly and dangerous. A world composed of an unending Miami or Calcutta or Djakarta, sick and stinking."

"People around here are getting more aware of it," Wade said. "I saw in the paper where the country loses a half million acres of wetlands a year. I went up the Escatawpa a couple of months ago, first time in years.

It's a mess up there. No grasses, dead cypress and a hell of a stench. Industrial pollution, they told me."

Hammond looked at his watch. "There's a four-fifteen flight I can make. I appreciate your trouble. And I understand your position in this: If and when you should ever need it, I can testify as to this meeting and what you gave me. But like I said, it isn't unusual. It's pretty typical. We get it all the time. I'll see that these reach the right hands."

"Here's something else that probably ought to go to the same people. It's just a list of all the county and state and federal permissions a person would have to get to build out there on Bernard. And I've put my guess as to the chance of getting them. You can see that after a lot of them I've put 'no chance at all.' Being a broker, I'm pretty well up on how hard it is to get permits."

"This ought to be useful too. Thanks. I'm glad I was able to come down and talk to you."

His mother told everybody that Lancelot's daddy was killed in Korea before Lancelot was born. It was easier to tell than the true story, and maybe easier for her boy to believe. But she was at last the only person left who called him Lancelot. He hated that name. He was determined to have people call him Bubba. He liked that name. He liked the warm, rough, friendly, dangerous sound of it. He called himself Bubba. He was big for his age, and he hammered a lot of kids into calling him Bubba. Bubba Davis.

Then one rainy afternoon in junior high, at a rehearsal in the auditorium, a teacher had called him

Lancelot, and he had bellowed from the stage, "Ever'body calls me Bubba!"

And Chuck Tyler, one of those he had tried to beat up and couldn't, yelled from the audience, "You ain't no Bubba, boy. You's a Booba!"

And, in time, he got used to being called Boob Davis, and even came to like it in a certain sense because it had become his costume. People expect a boob to be hearty and muscular and loud and witless. People appreciate a boob. A boob makes them feel smarter than they are, by comparison. They help you when they can. You laugh loudly at their jokes. You run and fetch things for people, like a happy dog. And people make allowances. They expect you to screw up. And that means you can take bigger risks, because when things don't work out, you're forgiven.

The offices of the Bernard Island Corporation were on the tenth floor of the West Bay Independent Bank Building, an almost new signature building on the northwest corner of Beach Boulevard and Twenty-third Street. Boob Davis was standing by the window wall in Tucker Loomis' office, looking out toward the Gulf.

"Swear to God, Tuck, I had to look out this thing ever' day, I'd sooner or later take a run at it. Makes me want to jump. You should maybe have a little railing outside there."

"So come over and sit down and tell me more."

Boob ambled over and swung a straight chair around and straddled it, resting his forearms on the chair back. "Nothing much more to tell. We've got the experts all lined up. Hydrologists, beach erosion guys,

hurricane construction specialists, desalinization figures, core samples, botanists, marine biologists, ecolo-
gists, sewage disposal people. We've got a rendering of
the whole island the way it would have looked, all in
color, like from two thousand feet up. Pretty damn
thing. He put in both clubs and about sixty houses and,
like you suggested, the big boat basin."

"Table model?"

"Be ready by next weekend. It's hinged in two
places so we can get it into the courtroom. And we've
got a nice slide show. I didn't like the sound track. I
think music was a bad idea. So it's going to be just
voice, and now the fellow from Sam's office that's
going to read it, he's got a dry boring voice. That's
what you should have in court so nobody thinks it's
some kind of jazz going on. Tell you the truth, I can't
think of one damn thing we've forgot. Not a one."

"I thought of one in the night."

"Like what?"

"Like you've got an average ten-foot depth in the
whole Sound, all eighty-something miles of it, and you
have got it shallowing off pretty good as you come up
on Bernard. I'd guess that on the north side of the
island, a hundred yards off the beach, you haven't got
more than three feet of depth. Barges would have to
come in to unload. That means a lot of ecofreaks
whimpering about the dredges covering up their pretty
green seaweed. And it would mean a lot of fussing
with the Corps of Engineers. So let's have a plan in
there that we were going to dredge the channel for the
barges and the yacht club and we were going to pipe it
way ashore, over to this low place here." Tuck turned

his chair and used a pencil to point to an area on the map on the wall behind his desk.

Boob had a big round face and a big high forehead. He hit himself in the forehead with the heel of his hand. "I should have thought of that. You are one smart man, Tuck. It makes another problem though. That's salt marsh. Protected wetlands."

"So find someplace else to put it! Jesus! Make a new dune somewhere. Get Cal to estimate total cubic yards of sand and figure out how big the dune would be, and get the son of a bitch on the rendering and on the table model."

"Okay. Sorry about that. I'll take care of it right off."

"Don't get up. You stay right here a minute."

"What's wrong?"

"I don't know if there *is* anything wrong. Are you still working on how to screw those two old country boys from Jackson out of that fifteen hundred acres out beyond Parklands?"

"I give it some thought now and then."

"Don't give it any more thought. Don't go rattling around the country trying to deal. I've been two years putting this island project together and I want it to go sweet and smooth and quick. And it seems to me that we've all been dividing our attention too damn much. Too many 'arns in the far,' as my daddy used to say. Nobody really minding the store. I don't know why I should be nervous but I am. What you do right now, you go back to the first piece of paper on this whole Bernard Island thing and you go through every sheet, every paragraph, every sentence and every word."

"Tuck, honest to God, that's just what Bobby Tom and Buddy over to Sam Loudner's office have been doing. And if they found a thing wrong with any of—"

"Boob, you're all the time talking when I'm talking to you. Just once in a while you ought to stand back until I ask you something."

"Sorry about that."

"Now I'm asking you. I knew Bobby Tom Schlesinger was going to represent us at the condemnation, but I thought Ray Humber was going to work with him. What happened?"

"Well, I guess it was Sam Loudner's decision, Tuck. Ray is going to leave the firm come the end of September. So not knowing the scheduling or knowing if there'll be an appeal, it seemed best to put Buddy Yoder on it. I guess Sam didn't check it with you because he knows you know how good Buddy is."

"So why didn't you check it with me, Boob?"

"On account of this is the first I knew Sam didn't tell you."

"Okay, okay. That's what I mean about things getting disorganized. We've got too damn much going on around here. I don't care if Buddy and Bobby Tom think everything is stone perfect. I want you doing just what I said—dropping everything else and reviewing everything we've got and everything we've done up 'til now. Can you do that for me?"

"Sure. No problem."

"How'd Buddy make out up in Washington?"

"He camped right on old Senator LaRue until finally some staff people took him over to Interior and got him in to see the right people and they decided it was within their guidelines and they let him have the permit and authorization."

"Should make Woody real happy."

"I hear it did."

"I'll tell Woody at poker Saturday night I heard the permit has been canceled. I like to see the way his eyes bug out. Now you can run along, Boob. But remember. No new games until we get this here condemnation award taken care of."

Boob hesitated. "I was just wondering."

"Wondering what?"

"You want me to go back and check over everything, right? But I don't think it would be such a good idea I go to Sam Loudner and ask him if it is all set that Judge Swane gets the case."

"God Almighty, Boob! The clerk of the court got two thousand dollars to make sure Swane sits on the case. You should know because you carried the money up there and handed it over. You trying to check on yourself? Trying to find out if you kept it or lost it?"

"I was just—"

"Get the hell out of here!"

Tucker Loomis got up and went to his window wall and looked down at the street. He saw the little figure of Boob Davis down there in his white suit walking around to the bank parking lot. The little figure swaggered. Tuck felt annoyed. 'That little ol' boy is just too cute. A boob he ain't. And I have the strong feeling he's been slicing off a little more than his share for a few years now. Little tricks. Little folk dances. Favors

for people I deal with in return for a little cash under
the table. Get this whole case off my mind and I'll
have to get into this and set him up. Prove it one way
or the other. Can't have people that cute around me.
When they see the chance to take a really big slice,
they take it and leave town.'

6

It was the fourth item in the inch-high stack of mail Wilbur Barley's secretary had put in the precise center of the blotter on his gray steel desk at ten after nine on Monday morning, the fourth day of August.

The small memorandum stapled to the top left corner had been handwritten by C. Perry McGuire himself. "Let me have your comment when convenient." No salutation, no signature.

The cover letter was from a Gordon Hammond and it was on National Park Serive letterhead and began "Dear Per." After some social chat about not seeing each other in such a long time, the letter went on to say, "The attached information came into my hands quite by accident. You will see that the deeds are for building sites on Bernard Island, which we have laid claim to and are preparing to pay for. I am not free to

disclose the name of my informant, but he assures me
that these four chaps are quite unable to pay those
prices for land, and they are all employed in somewhat
menial capacities by one Mr. Tucker Loomis, who is
president and principal stock owner of the Bernard Island Corporation, and is a resident of West Bay, as are
all four of the alleged land buyers.

"The second piece of information is a list of the permits and certifications that any developer of Bernard
Island would be quite unable to secure, according to
my informant. I want to assure you that he is a knowl-
edgeable person in these areas.

"I know that you remember as I do the outrageous
price we had to pay for that addition to Annabelle
Forest three years ago, when we faced a similar 'rip-
off' conspiracy and could do nothing about it. So I
offer these bits of information not out of any desire to
meddle, but in hopes they will be of some use to your
people when this action comes before the Court. For-
give me for not sending them through channels as
They tell us we should, but we both know that had I
done so, you would have received them long after the
whole affair was over and done."

Wilbur Barley studied the four deeds and the list of
certifications and permits. He dropped the correspondence into the bottom right drawer of his desk and
kicked the drawer shut. He felt very warm, and then
he felt chilly. A shivering sensation had begun deep
inside of him, between belly and backbone. His hands
were steady. His breathing was steady. He took his
pulse. It felt normal. But the shivering was there. It
was somewhat like excitement. Like the excitement of

seeing that little boat down there when he and Harry had flown over it and circled back to land. It was a little bit like the shivering excitement he felt whenever he headed for the Grand Jury Room, folders under his arm, knowing he had an absolute lock on the miscreant, an inevitable indictment, conviction and sentence. But that shivering had a nucleus of pleasure in it, a hidden little chunk of warm. This was total chill and silence, wrapped in shivering.

He took the men's room key out of his middle drawer and walked past he ticking and buzzing and humming of Miss Wargrove's computer terminal, out the door and down the corridor. He stood at the urinal to no avail and remembered he had been there a little before nine. He washed his hands thoroughly, and then examined himself in the mirror. He looked as he always looked. He took his gold-rimmed glasses off and polished them. He adjusted the blonde bangs that lay across his forehead. He smoothed the wings of the small blonde mustache and noticed that he had taken a fraction of a millimeter too much off the left side.

He tried to make himself think about going in and talking to C. Perry McGuire. But he could not make his mind approach that eventuality. It kept darting back and away and off to the side, off into past pastures, the green groves of youth. It hustled onto a ship going through the Gatun Locks. It took him into a randy bed with an accidental woman who giggled endlessly. It took him up to the roof of the old Federal Building and together he and it looked down into the street, and that was strange because he had never been on the roof. But he could not make it walk with him into McGuire's office. He could not even visualize McGuire or his office.

"I am a good man," the inner voice said. "I have always been a good man. I have done things that were not worthy of me. But they were little things. I regret them. But no big things. Yet. So standing here, I am still good. I am okay. See me in the mirror? I can smile. I can wink. I can straighten my tie. I can put my shoulders back. I can stay in here all day if I want to."

An August hurricane came up the Gulf, stalled, and then went whistling and booming over into Mexico, the eye coming ashore at less than hurrican velocity just south of Matamoros. It blew down a few thousand signs in Brownsville and Harlingen, thus performing an esthetic service to Gulf Coast Texas. Fishing was superb on the grass flats inside the Chandeleurs, with big catches of what the locals call spec, the Floridians call speckled trout and the East Coasters call weakfish. A few hard rains fell on the drought areas, running off so quickly from the guttered land that not enough of it nourished the aquifer.

On a Wednesday afternoon, August twentieth, fifteen men at a boardroom table littered with cups and beers and ashtrays and the remnants of lunch, finally agreed to a buyout price of nineteen dollars and fifty cents per share for Maxim Engineering, with Cordray Communications paying ten cash and the balance in a new class of Cordray preferred which carried with it a common stock warrant to buy the common stock at any time up to five years at twenty dollars a share.

News of the agreement dropped Cordray from sixteen to fourteen before the closing bell.

Two days later the usual foursome holed out at Londleaf a little after five and buzzed Jerry to bring them their customary beverages in the locker room. After they'd changed and Billy DeVine and Doc Crocker had driven on home, Stu Persons and Judge D. Henry Swane went into the men's bar. They talked for a time about the game, and shook their heads over Doc's eagle on the fourteenth. By rights the ball should have gone across the green, across the trap and into the shrubbery. But it had wedged itself, on the fly, between the pin and the side of the cup.

Stu Persons, the contractor, was a medium-height, thick, broad brown man with no waist, no neck and a basso profundo voice. He left his half-drink and made a phone call from the telephone at the end of the bar, came back and said, "I guess we got out of that about right, Henry."

"Down?"

"Closed on the low for the day. How much Maxim you say you bought?"

"I didn't say. Not much. A few hundred shares."

Persons smiled to himself. Woody had called him from West Bay last month to see if he could find out how much the Judge had gone for. No great problem. He had a good contact at the stockbrokers where the Judge maintained an account. Swane had put in a limited buy order and gotten twelve hundred shares at eight, then moved it up to eight and five-eighths and gotten nine hundred at eight and a half and three hundred at eight and five-eighths. He had made his last buy at nine, two thousand shares, and all of it margined. He had bought it all during the week of July twentieth. Forty-four hundred shares which had cost him almost thirty-eight thousand plus brokerage commission. And he knew the Judge had started moving out at eighteen, and then nineteen, and closed out the balance at twenty. So call it eighty-four thousand less commissions. And call it a forty-five thousand short-term gain, or probably about thirty after taxes. When he had reported by phone, Woody had said that the Judge's good fortune would make some other people happy too. It was agreed that the Judge was a nice fellow. He deserved the best.

Bern Gibbs was on time for his eleven a.m. appointment with Tucker Loomis out at the Loomis house in the Parklands development. He parked on the long curve of the driveway and went into the entry atrium and heard the faint sound of chimes inside the house when he touched the bell button. A panel was pushed aside in the top half of the door and a middle-aged woman looked at him and said, "Yes?"

"My name is Gibbs. Mr. Loomis is expecting me."

"Just a moment, please."

After he had waited for several minutes, Loomis came around the side of the house, shouldering into a yellow shirt. He wore dark blue shorts and white deck shoes with the laces missing.

"Hey, Bern. Sure glad you could shake loose on a Saturday morning. Appreciate it. Let's drive on out to the back gate. What kind of car is this here?"

"BMW, Tuck."

"Kind of a cute little thing. Me, I like bigger cars. Look, you just head on out that way, and when we get to Mockingbird Lane, turn left and go to the end."

Bernard Gibbs parked, and after Tuck opened the gate they walked along a path that led east and north, climbing gradually until they were at the top of a knoll, high enough to overlook piney woods and brushlands and the curve of a stream filled by the rains. "What maybe we can do," Tuck said, "is pick up a little bit more than fifteen hundred more acres, shaped like an L. So it runs across this five hundred way there to the east, and then comes around and up against our boundaries to the north of us here. We're working on it. Now you tell me what you think about when you think of how we ought to go ahead on this whole two-thousand-acre addition to Parklands."

Bern felt as if there wasn't quite enough room in his chest for his heart, and certainly not enough room for a deep breath. "I would say you and your people should go absolutely first class. What I'm saying is that the yacht and tennis club and the golf and country club you built for the first phase are more than big enough to take care of the first phase of Parklands even after it's completely sold out. I think maybe the theme here should be nature. Keep ever stick of hardwood we can. Make the roads match the terrain. Off there to the southwest where I would guess from here you might have the least desirable construction areas, some shortsighted developers might think in terms of town-house condominium but that, to me, would degrade the whole project. No, I would say use those areas for nature walks, jogging, maybe stables and horse barns. Lean heavy on big tracts, security, natural values."

"Are there enough people with that kind of money?"

"Nobody can stop this area growing. A whole third of this nation is going to be packed around Florida and the Gulf Coast. And for every ten couples that come in here with enough for a fifty-thousand-dollar condo, there'll be one comes in with the extra zero tacked on for a house and lot at Parklands."

"I like the way you think, Bern. I like the way your mind works. I think maybe we'll be able to do business out here, you and me and Wade. I think we can make a piece of money. These gnats are getting to me. Let's head on back to the house."

They sat in the shade out by the big screened pool behind Tuck's house. Tuck fixed Bloody Marys, strong.

"Of course," he said, "a lot depends on this Bernard Island thing coming out favorable. You can understand that."

"Sure. I realize that."

"Lots of times a man needs to fix himself a little edge. You know what I mean? A man has to make sure folks are going to look at him favorable in a court of law. So I kind of tried to make sure that the folks working on the condemnation proceedings in the District Court wouldn't climb up onto any white horses and go after any holy grails. I tried to make sure it wouldn't be taken too serious. I set me up a kind of friendship with the people on the other side. Quiet like. And as far as I know, Bern, it was all set and I could lay back and wait it out with my mind at rest. You follow?"

"Yes sir."

"Well, not too long ago I got a confidential phone call from my friend over there and he was upset all to hell. He says that somebody give a Park Service fellow name of Hammond copies of four of the deeds processed in your office, and this Hammond gave them to the top man in his office, along with the news that not one of those four could afford the land they signed up for. What do you say to that?"

"All we did, Tuck, all we were supposed to do, was process the mortgage deeds according to the fact sheets—"

"Don't tell me stuff I already know. I want to know what you think about this man hammond being given those deeds."

"They're recorded. That means that the public has access—"

"Warner Ellenson checked that out for me. The clerk down there says nobody made copies from the public records, and that means they had to come from your real estate agency."

"I don't see how you can say that for sure."

"I can say that for sure, Gibbs, because I checked out every single damn one of my people that had a chance to lay a hand on those deeds at any time, and every damn one of them knows that if they snuck around behind my back, I'd pull their fucking lips off. So it was your outfit for sure. Along with them was a list of the permits and certificates somebody thinks I would never be able to get if I tried to go ahead with

Bernard Island. Now what that does, Bern, it makes those folks sit up and take notice. It makes them think old Tuck is running some kind of skin game down here. The government gets touchy about skin games. They want to be on the side of virtue and God and chastity and all that shit. Follow me?"

"I guess so."

"Your hand was a little shaky when you hoisted that glass, and I guess that's the way I want you to be. Just a little bit shaky, Bern. This fellow, the one that was going to make sure they didn't go after this condemnation hammer and tongs, I gave him a little present in front and it was all set that after it all comes out nice, he would get another little present, and he was going to work his little ass off to make sure he got this second present. But Hammond scared the pee out of him. Now he tells me he can't do what he thought he could do. He says he doesn't want to touch it with an eleven-foot pole. But he'll try to do what I want him to do because I got leverage on him. I got him right by his little pink balls. And he says he only went over what was going on at this end. I thought so too, Bern. I thought that when I put it in your hands, everything was under control. Maybe I was wrong about you all along. What do you say?"

"I don't know what to say."

"I took you up on the hilltop, my friend, and I showed you a piece of the golden future that could all be yours. Let me make something else clear. Unless we work this out, you and me, in a way that satisfies me, not only are you not going to have anything more to do with Parklands ever, but you are not going to do much business of any kind in West Bay or anywhere near West Bay. No bank is going to go along with any deal you try to set up. I'm not a vindictive fella, Bern. I just feel that deceit and disloyalty should be punished."

"Jesus Christ, Tuck!"

"I better be Mr. Loomis until we get this worked out, Gibbs."

"What is there to work out?"

"Haven't you been listening? There is a cold breeze blowing on my ass. There is a chance that my friend at court will get his balls back in running condition and he'll do just like he promised in the beginning. But suppose he don't. I'm going to be there in court looking like a dummy when they bring up these deeds to Ezra Feeney, Jack Simms, Dutch Stanfield and Frankie Phipps. Those four all work for me. What can happen in court that can make me smile and smile? Take a guess."

"Uh . . . it turns out they have enough money to buy the land?"

"Wrong."

"Oh! It turns out we have no record of those deeds?"

"You're getting warm."

"But how can you handle the recording—"

"Didn't that little girl of yours, that Dawn Marina—"

"Marino."

"Anyway, Marina Marino, the one you get to screw every once in a while at the Waveland Motel."

"I guess I shouldn't ask how you know that."

"No, you shouldn't ask, but I'll tell you. When I wondered if it could be you jerking me around, I had some people look into your lifestyle, and they come up with this Dawn woman. Anyway, she did the notarizing?"

"The deeds all came back to the office with the signatures of the principals and the witnesses and they came back all notarized in your office. She took them down for recording."

"But she is a notary public?"

"Yes."

"And you tell her to notarize a blank sheet of paper, she'll do it, won't she?"

"Yes sir. I guess so."

"Be sure, damn it. Will she?"

"Yes sir."

"I don't think we'll have to use her for anything at all. But the two of you, you and Dawn, you got to get any trace of those deeds and sales out of your office and off your records. So you make that little lady notarize some blank sheets and you hide them away and when she asks about them, which she will, you just smile mysterious. Can you do that? I just want to know she'll be there if we need her. What we'll do on those four, we'll make up a new set of originals and we'll have somebody else sign as notary, and I'll have some other people sign the names of Phipps and Feeney and Simms and Stanfield. The witnesses will be some people that don't exist. I can guaran-goddamn-tee you that those boys that work for me will have no memory at all of buying any land. Warner will make sure the copies in the court house get switched. You take care of your office and I'll take care of everything else, and then if it comes up at the proceedings, it is going to look like a plot against me, like some clumsy kind of shit cooked up by the ecofreaks."

"There's a lot of loose ends, Tu—Mr. Loomis."

"So you and me, we clip off every one we can find. And what you have to do—and this is important—is to keep your mouth shut. Let whoever tried to screw me think they're getting away with it. That's important. Maybe it won't ever have to come out if my little friend gets hisself back on the track. But if he doesn't, I want to be ready to run a counterplay. Is that clear?"

A woman came out of the house and cleared her throat. "Is there anything else I can do? The nurse has had her lunch. Your lunch is on the table, sir."

"That's all, Lottie. Thanks. Have a nice weekend."

"Thank you, sir."

After she left, Tucker Loomis said, "I shouldn't be too hard on you, Bern. After all, this whole screw-up is my fault. I make dumb mistakes because I don't think things through. It was sort of a half-joke to sign up those four to buy lots on Bernard. Every other purchaser can damn well afford his lots."

"I . . . I hope it all works out."

"You run along now, Bern. Like they say, don't call me, I'll call you. Just clean it up fast."

Tuck Loomis got up and stretched and listened to the snarl of Gibbs' little BMW heading away into the early afternoon. He went into the abrupt coolness of the air-conditioned house and padded back to Thelma's room and looked in on her again. Maria had cranked her bed back down and Thelma was having her afternoon nap. She made a bubbling sound with her lips at each exhalation.

He went to the kitchen alcove and took the plastic wrap off the bowl of salad Lottie had fixed for him, and took his glass of iced tea out of the refrigerator. It was a Greek salad with a lot of feta cheese, the way he liked it, and he added a trace of oil and vinegar.

After he put the empty salad bowl and glass in the sink, he went looking for Maria and found her sitting cross-legged on the end of his bed, looking at the small television screen on the bookshelf. She grinned at him. The whiteness of her teeth and the whiteness of the whites of her eyes against that golden skin always startled and pleased him. He shucked off his shirt and stepped out of his shorts and stretched out behind her.

As he began stroking her, she said, "Hey. Wait a minute. I want to see how this comes out."

He stretched out and hitched over to the side so that he could see the screen. The woman was standing at the edge of a cliff. The sea was smashing against the rocks. The man came up to her and she turned and smiled at him. There was a close shot of their long hungry kiss, and the man said it would be forever and the woman said she never had any doubts and, as they walked down the curving path from the clifftop, the credits began to scroll down the screen. Maria hopped up and punched the set off, and turned to him, glowing, and said, "That was beautiful. It was really beautiful, Tuck."

"Everything is beautiful, sweet thing," he said, and she took her uniform off and hung it on a chair, sat on the chair and took off her white nurse shoes and her white socks. She put her brassiere and panties on top of her dress, and reached to take off the little starched white cap.

"Hey, leave the cap on," he said.

"You want me with it on? It's real old-fashioned. Hardly anybody wears even the uniform anymore. Okay, so it stays on."

She came and put one round shiny knee on the bed and said, "Well, look at you!"

"I've been thinking about you, kid."

"I like Saturdays. I really like Saturdays a lot," she said, smiling, and lowered herself upon him with delicacy and precision.

Wilbur Barley stopped at the Sunset Nursing Facility to look in on his sister on his way home. She was in a room at the back on the ground floor. The only window looked out upon the service entrance and a big blue dumpster. If she couldn't look out the window, she didn't need a view. She could open and close her eyes. She could breathe. She could swallow the gruel they spooned into her. One could say it was an improvement over the months of tubes and intravenous drips. She was as white and soft as suet. There had been some trouble with bed sores, and some trouble about keeping her hair washed and brushed, until finally Barley lost patience and had a talk with the administrator, promising to do his best to have the state investigators take a closer look at SNF with a view to lifting the license. Now the care had improved. Unguents and massage. A better balancing of diet to keep her from getting any bigger. They had explained the last encephalogram to him. Not totally flat. A little bit of activity. But no essential change from the previous one.

He stood by the foot of the bed and stared down at Carol. She was a year younger than he was. Thirty-six. She and harry had tried for years to have kids. Finally adopted one and when it was two years old it fell off the upstairs porch onto the edge of a brick planter and died. And Carol and Harry started drinking a little too much, and when she fell in the tub and hit her head she was drunk. Harry contributed all he could afford, a hundred and fifty a week. The rest of it was eating Wilbur up. He was confused. What good was she? She could live another thirty years. In order to support a corpse, keep it clean and plump, he had entered into an arrangement with Mr. Loomis. When they were plugged into something, you could pull the plug. These people would not stop feeding her. She was money in the bank. This thing on the bed wasn't Carol. So what was it? The soul had fled. It was an unburied body. You could not get public assistance if you owned property and made a good salary. She was his only close blood relation. Sister. There was a welter of Christmas-card relatives over in Georgia. No help at all there.

Close the door behind him. Gently squeeze the nostrils together, place the palm of the other hand firmly and carefully over the pallid lips. It would be so easy. Thirteen hundred and twenty-five a month. Less Harry's six hundred. Seven hundred and twenty-five divided into . . . So the other half of the money from Loomis would mean he could stop thinking about it for an additional batch of years. There was a box of Kleenex on the nightstand. He snuffled and wiped his eyes, looked at her again and left.

Harry was in the little lounge near the front door. Wilbur was surprised to see him there.

"You could have come up while I was there."

"I wanted to see you, Wil, not her."

"What about?"

"I don't go in there and look at her anymore. What's the point? I haven't seen her in six months. I hate to have to tell you this, but we've all had to take a voluntary cut at the plant, all the middle-management people. Our taking a cut is the only way they can get the union to agree to their cuts. So I got to cut back on this too. I can't swing it anymore. Four hundred a month. That's all I can do. Sorry."

"You're her husband."

"And you're her brother. So?"

"My God, Harry! What am I supposed to do?"

"Are we supposed to be doing this? Is it some kind of sacred obligation or something? You're the lawyer. You tell me. We walk away from it, what can they do? Sue?"

"I can't do that."

"If the whole thing was up to me, I would. But as long as you're hanging in, I'll do what I can. But it will have to be less from now on."

7

Wade sat at his desk looking at the brochures from the state capital. They were intended to promote tourism, to entice permanent residents and to lure industry. All real estate brokers were on the state's mailing list.

The color photographs and the self-conscious text created a Mississippi he had never known. All the miles of empty sandy beaches, pretty girls under bright beach umbrellas, tours of the old plantation houses with the hostesses in hoop skirts, the million acres of national forests—DeSoto, Holly Springs, Bienville, Tombigbee and Homochitto—with pretty girls standing under flowering magnolia trees, pretty girls water-skiing, pretty girls smiling and holding armloads of azaleas, camellias and Cherokee roses. Pretty girls in skiffs holding up specs and mackerel and giant shrimp to be admired.

West Bay still had some of the old houses fronting on West Beach Road, big old frame mansions showing the French and Spanish colonial influence. Only a few left. Helen Yoder had just sold one of them for a nice dollar. And there were a few of the narrow pedestrian alleys left in the old part of downtown.

But what they were trying to sell seemed to him to be the Mississippi of 1950, when he was three years old. Nowadays Route 90 had gutted the whole fifty-four miles of Gulf coast, and I-55 and 10 and 110 and 20 had carved up the old land soaked long ago by the blood of Nate Forrest's troopers. Another brochure picture showed the line of cheerleaders, hopping and screaming for Ole Miss, an obligatory scene in all state propaganda.

What they didn't show and would never talk about were all the ratty little decayed businesses beside the boom of traffic, grass high in what had been parking lots, derelict signs a-dangle. Mountains of trash and garbage leaching poisons into the aquifer. Teen gangs prowling the shadows of the night streets, grabbing and snatching. And another kind of garbage leaking into the ears, loud thumpety rock and country, rackety roar of the trucks, organized inanity of cable and network, and the yelping and keening of patrol car and ambulance once the sun had set.

But if you leave the coastal zone and go on up through the long silences of the piney woods, you had a choice of the two Mississippis that do not invite the preparation of brochures—the great Delta, the alluvial plain which extends down the whole west edge of the state, or the great East Gulf Coastal Plain, punctuated by the Loess Hills, the Tombigbee, the Natchez Trace. He remembered the strange beauty of the rolling country near the prairie, the deep and narrow stream valleys coming off the stunted hills. Too many people, he thought. Too many of them swarming in here, changing everything. They have to have their malls and their pizza places, their motels and high-rises and their little automatic banks on every corner. They have to go out on the piers to the seafood restaurants and eat the frozen fish flown in here from South Africa.

Suddenly his indignation amused him and he tossed the brochures aside. Such attitudes on the part of a real estate salesman could be called terminal disloyalty, punishable by having to attend a year of conventions. He would give the brochures to the next pilgrims hoping to buy a house near the beach. They could go looking for the pretty girls. They would find huge flaccid women on the beach, their wobbling tissues scorched pink by the indifferent sun, whining at their scrawny macho husbands and backhanding their kids. Ask *them* what happened to the pretty girls of yesteryear.

Ellie Service came in, looking troubled. "Got a minute, Wade?" He nodded and she closed the door behind her and sat across from him. "Something weird is going on."

"Every day. It's a chronic disease."

"No, I mean more than usual. I have to background it for you."

"You sound like Dan Rather. Go ahead."

"Little by little, Jeanie Nash has been teaching me

111

to run that PC out there. I'm not up to communications yet, with the modem and all that. But I can dig into our files that are on hard disk and get what I want and print it out. It isn't as difficult as Jeanie makes out, but I can see why she wants to keep it all mysterious. Anyway, yesterday, Monday, because it was the first day of September, I wanted a client list for the last three months. You've seen the list. It's alphabetical by client, with the contract date and amount, a code for the kind of property. It's simple, one line per buyer and one line per seller. As you know, this isn't the greatest year we've ever had, so it isn't a long list. A page and a half. With holes in it. I mean places where there were no names. Four of them. Here is the printout. Take a look."

Puzzled, he looked at the list. The first hole came between Faminger, Mr. and Mrs. Robert E., and Feeney, Mr. and Mrs. Horace T. He realized at once that Feeney, Ezra, would have fitted nicely in the blank space. He checked and saw that there were alphabetical spaces for Simms and Stanfield and Phipps. The four who had flunked finance.

"Somebody deleted them?"

"It wasn't me and it wasn't Jeanie. Jeanie had already taught me that when you delete items from a list, you use a deletion protocol that causes the rest of the names to hitch up a space and fill the holes. If you just use the delete key, it leaves a hole. Somebody had called that file up onto the screen and edited it by deleting those four names and then put it back onto the disk. It was yesterday that I got into this with Jeanie. She has a program she runs every night before she

112

leaves. What it does it put any new stuff on the hard disk onto tape, so if the hard disk crashes, she can rebuild it from the tape backup."

"Whatever that means."

"She pulled the same file of clients from the tape she made Friday night, and printed it out. Here. See, the missing names are still on the list. And this morning the names are gone, so somebody got in here over the weekend and deleted the names, not even knowing there was backup and not even knowing how to reform the file after deletions."

"What did she do about it?"

"She talked to Frank Mettler after I talked to her. She hadn't locked the computer, not in months. He told her to put the missing names back into the file and lock it from now on. Anyway, I checked out the cross-indexed file cards, and the client cards and contract cards and closing cards for these four accounts are gone. Completely. Vanished."

"I have the uneasy feeling I know why."

"Why?"

"You noticed that these four were all Bernard Island sales?"

"Yes, of course."

"All I can say right now, Ellie, is maybe they weren't real sales."

She pursed her lips and studied her thumbnail for what seemed a long time, then said, "So that makes it something for you to straighten out with Bern, doesn't it?"

"Yes it surely does."

"Then good luck."

Bern was out. Dawn Marino said he would be back about two in the afternoon, but probably later because it was an Ole Miss Alumni Lunch at the West Bay Hyatt.

So he asked her if he could look at the list of the Bernard Island sales. She hesitated, then slid the file drawer of her desk open and pulled the file and handed it to him. It had a fresh feel and look. It was a typed list rather than a computer printout. And there were thirty-five names on it instead of thirty-nine.

He handed it back to her and said, "Thanks."

"You're welcome," she said and slipped the list back into the file. She straightened up and as he stood there, looking at her, she lifted her chin slightly and narrowed her eyes. 'I've got it good,' her stare said, 'and don't try to mess it up.'

He smiled at her. 'I'm going to give it my best shot, sweetie,' he was saying with his gaze.

"Please take a note to Bern, Dawn. See that he gets it when he comes in. I won't have to hang around and sign it. Here's how it goes: Please stay past five-thirty, Bern, and I'll meet you then in your office. There's a lot to talk about, and it is very important."

Jack Simms, the dockmaster at Parklands, was living aboard the *Stress Test*, a Harbor Master forty-seven-foot houseboat owned by Dr. George Peabody. The Doctor and his wife and children were due back from Sweden in November. Jack had asked old Feeney to stop on by when he got off gate duty at six. The sun was still hot when Ezra Feeney parked his rusty old truck in the lot and came out to the houseboat at the end of B dock. Jack had the ice bucket, the water jug, one of the Doctor's quarts of Wild Turkey and the two glasses on a small table on the port deck, out of sight of the other boats and the yacht club property.

After they had talked about the heat and had most of their first drink, Jack said, "Well, what did you think of it?"

"I'll tell you, by God, I didn't think a hell of a lot of it. I never in my life had a grown-up white man talk to me like that. I wouldn't talk to a nigger the way he talked to me."

"Ol' Tuck, he was upset. I seen him that mad only one time before and that was last year when an Alabama boat came in too fast and thumped him one, busted some splinters off that fancy transom."

"He had no call to talk to me like that. I didn't want to buy land on his goddman island. He told me to and I did. Now I got to forget it ever happened because if I just happen to remember at the wrong time, he is going to see my balls get nailed to a stump. Why was he yelling?"

"Because that's the way he is sometimes."

"It's ugly. Plain damn ugly."

"Go ahead. Pour your own. You got to understand it from his side, Ezra. He's got a big thing going with that island and all, and he was just kidding around, having four of us without a pot to pee in sign deeds for expensive land. The way these developers do, they try to make things look real active. Like you got a little restaurant, you get your friends to park in front so it looks busy. He wanted to have lots of deeds so it would look like lots of sales going on. He wanted lots

115

of sales because he had a dream about that island. He was going to turn it into the luxury spot of the whole world. A millionaires' paradise. It was going to be in all the magazines. And then those rotten Park Service bastards come along and grab the island. So now he's trying to get compensated. And he's afraid those deeds of ours he put in like a joke, they'll spoil it for him. The judge might think he's trying to fix up a lot of deeds so he can get more money back from the feds."

"I still don't like any man talking to me the way he talked."

"He talked to me the same way."

"I don't care how he talked to you or anybody else. It's me I'm talking about. I plain didn't like it."

"What pissed him off, Feeney, is how one of the real estate fellows he was working with, that man went to the Court and finked on him, told the Court there were four bad deeds out, yours and mine and a couple others. So it's important they come up with subpoenas, we don't know a damn thing. Never bought nothing, never signed nothing. All the paperwork has been chucked out. They even snuck the certified copies out of the court house, out of the county clerk's files."

Feeney fixed a new drink and turned slowly and stared at Simms. "You say it was a real estate man went to the Court?"

"Somebody from Rowley/Gibbs."

"A fellow from that company came to my place and told me maybe I could get ten thousand dollars for giving up my claim on my land out on that island."

"No shit! When was this?"

"Back sometime maybe late July. Set on a bench at

my place and I give him a cold beer. He was born here. Nice to talk to."

"You ask me, Feeney, I'd say he was a scumbag. He got you to tell him you didn't have enough money to buy the land."

"I didn't think it meant anything. Shit, he showed me a list of names and asked if I knew anybody on it that couldn't pay for the land either, and I said I knew you and you sure couldn't buy that kind of land for the prices in the deed."

"You better not let Tuck know about it."

"Why not?"

"If he was trying to get Tuck jammed up, maybe he had one of those little tape recorders on him."

"Now I wouldn't take that too kindly, Mr. Simms."

"What could you do about it now?"

"I guess I could leave a message he should come see me at my place, and then I could purely beat the shit out of him. He's got a good size on him, so maybe you could be there too and help out."

"I kind of like the thought of that, Mr. Feeney. I really do."

"I've been looking for him to come here since he came to see me, but he hasn't showed up when I've been on the gate. Yes, thank you, I do think I will have another piece of that good stuff there, Jack."

"You got to drive home. I'm home."

"Mr. Simms, I discovered a great secret long ago. When you see two of everything, like two sets of head-lights coming at you, when you close one eye and hold it shut, then there is only one of everything and you can keep out of the way. Don't worry about me."

117

"I think Mr. Loomis might appreciate us doing the right thing. It isn't the kind of thing he can do for hisself. What's the man's name?"

"It's on a card back at the trailer, a card he give me."

"I'll tell you something. Right now here in the twilight, it's a good idea. Knocking a scumbag around is a kind of a duty, you know. But the ideas that look good when you see them through bourbon, sometimes they don't look so great the next morning."

"Son of a bitch lied to me about that ten thousand dollars!"

"Don't ge too worked up. We can't do a thing tonight."

"All my life, people been lying to me. It's time I up and put a stop to it once and for all."

"That's right, Tiger."

When Wade came back to the office at five-thirty that Tuesday, Bern couldn't see him right away because he was in the middle of dictating a long memo for Ms. Marino to type, and he didn't want to interrupt his train of thought. It was a complicated matter, a new high-rise bank building contemplated for the corner of Edgewater Avenue and Twenty-third, with an arcade, a restaurant, twenty specialty shops and an additional sixty-five thousand square feet of office space to lease. When Wade came back an hour later, Bern was at his desk, scowling, reading the memo, marking it up with a red pencil.

"Jesus Christ!" he said. "Know how that twit spells *systems*? Ess-I-ess-tee-ee-em-ess!"

"One assumes she has other talents."

"You being a smartass?"

"Not today. Believe me, not today."

Bern stared at him and then pushed the long memo over to the side of his desk. "I've been trying to hold it in all day yesterday and today."

"Hold what in?"

"Don't give me that look of fucking angelic innocence, chum. You went behind my back, you son of a bitch! You ferreted out those four dummy contracts and you went to Hammond with them, and he went right to the U.S. Attorney!"

Wade raised his eyebrows. "That's very interesting! It means Tuck Loomis has somebody right in the office of the U.S. Attorney for this district. Somebody that keeps him up-to-date."

"And if you'd known that, you wouldn't have gotten cute."

"I would have done just what I did."

"You don't deny it?"

"Of course not!"

"You did it behind my back!"

"Talking to you face-to-face didn't work out, Bern."

"Jesus, you got a rotten attitude about this. What the hell are you trying to do? Kill us off? Kill the firm dead? I was with Loomis out at Parklands on Saturday."

"I know."

"Yes, I guess I told you. Told somebody. Anyway, what you don't realize s that this little Chapter S corporation can't exist without Loomis."

"It has for a long time."

119

"Not anymore, chum. Not from here on. He knows the information came out of this office. He thinks we stabbed him in the back. He says that if he comes out of the condemnation suit healthy, we can put together the whole sales program for the next two thousand acres out at Parklands. And if he gets bitched in the suit because of something leaking out of this firm, then we are never going to put together another deal in this area that requires a bank loan, because no bank is going to accept any paper when we're the broker involved."

"And you bought that kind of shit from him?"

"What kind of a world are you living in lately, Rowley? I'm talking about the real world here. Loomis told me not to say a word to anybody about this whole thing. I think I've got it taken care of."

"Not really," Wade said.

"What the hell is that supposed to mean?"

"It means you ain't got it took care of. We've got diligent loyal people working here. Somebody came in over the weekend and scrambled the records. I assume it was you and Miz Tits Marino. She must have some elementary knowledge of the IBM PC AT computer. She did a rotten job of erasing those four names from the client list. She left empty spaces, which is like sending up flares. Ellie came to me with the problem after she had talked it over with Jeanie. Jeanie took the problem to Frank Mettler and he told her to rebuild the file from the backup tapes and keep the computer locked at night from now on. This morning Ellie checked all the cards cross-filed by client and type of sale and so on, and she found that all the cards on

120

those four transactions had been lifted. We're gradually eliminating the card files themselves, but that's another story. Anyway, I decided that if you were coming in here and stealing files by night, it was time we had some serious conversation."

Bern's face was screwed into a strange disharmony, a most odd expression. He buried his head in his arms on the desktop, and for an unreal moment Wade thought the man was laughing. But he was stifling sobs. He got up quickly and spun away from the desk, mopping his face with his handkerchief.

"I've tried so goddamn hard," Bern said in a soft voice. "It's down the tube. All the way down."

"Look, the man is a blowhard, partner."

Bern came over and leaned his fist on the corner of the desk so that he could bend close to Wade's face. "I hate you, Rowley. Every one of these past three or four years I've hated you more. I don't know when it started or how it started. I hate your bland dumb face, and the lazy way you float around, and I hate your magazine-story marriage and your fairy-tale wife and kids. I hate the way everybody that works for us tries to break their ass to keep you happy. I hate the way you turn your back on the realities of the business world. Most of all I guess I hate doing eighty percent of the work and bringing in eighty percent of the money and collecting fifty percent of the net."

Wade looked up into that taut twisted face, into the reddened eyes, and had the sudden conviction that the man was in some unexpected way quite mad. But at the same time he felt a sense of relief. There had been quarrels, but none like this. And there had been a lot of other things which were now swept away. The back-yard steaks while the kids played, the shared triumph at deals which worked out well, the shared anxieties of the early days when they first started out. Gibbs/Rowley or Rowley/Gibbs? The first was alphabetical, the second easier to say. Bern had pulled the short straw.

"If you'd look at the books, Bern, you'd know that eighty percent figure is nonsense."

"So call it seventy then."

"If anything, it would be closer to sixty."

"So is that fair to me?"

You like to go out there like the Lone Ranger and cut deals by yourself so you can pull commission. But lots of times, pal, you have screwed up because you haven't had enough backup. Sometimes I've been able to save those deals of yours. Not too often, though. I have bird-dogged deals and brought in our own people in the beginning, and cut up the commission schedule. This isn't any big secret around here, Bern. Everybody knows how you like to work. You like to join the clubs and sing along and take three-hour lunches and fuck up the deals we could have brought home. And this Loomis mess is just another of your fuck-ups. So don't hang over me and glare. Okay?"

"You son of a bitch!" Bern whispered and swung at Wade's face. Wade ducked away from it and the fist hit him just above the left ear, a painful blow that dazed him for a moment. Bern Gibbs went dancing around the office, bent forward from the waist, holding his right hand against his belly.

He stopped and straightened and looked at his right hand. "I think I broke it," he said in a wondering tone.

"You had another of those long lunches today," Wade said. "And you are still sloshed." He reached and picked up the memorandum Bern had been marking and read some of it and put it back on the desk. "This is a lot of mush, Bern. The words sound important but there is no meaning. What depreciation schedule? What zoning restriction? These people want faces, not a lot of important sounds."

"I want you out!"

"*You* want *me* out? What is that supposed to mean?"

"I mean I want this partnership ended!"

"Rick Riker drew up the papers to begin it and he'll draw them up to end it. I agree. After this little scene, Bern, there's no way we can go on. But it makes lots of problems. Let me point out a couple. We each have fifty percent of the stock. The mechanics for appraisal of the value of the whole corporation are spelled out. Let's for the hell of it say the value including the equity in the building comes to one million. So I have to pay you fifty thousand a year for ten years or you have to pay me."

"I'm going to keep on running this business!"

"Great! But what if Loomis makes sure there isn't any business left?"

"That would be your fault, wouldn't it?"

"What difference whose fault? If you hadn't been so anxious to kiss his ass, we wouldn't be in any trouble."

"You got in touch with Hammond. Okay, what's done is done. But are you going to keep on trying to screw things up?"

"What do you mean?"

123

"I don't know. You've got this kind of death wish. Are you going to write letters to the papers? Or give an interview to your old buddy, Brud Barnes?"

"I did what I felt I had to do in order to try to clean our skirts, Bern. I can't think of anything else at the moment. If I think of something, I'll probably do it."

"That's a big help."

"Do you want my advice?"

"Not particularly."

"We have hereby agreed we are going to split. We don't have to decide who buys who out just yet. We should keep going as we are until this Loomis mess shakes down. Then we'll know where we're at."

Bern thought it over. He was cradling his right hand. "That makes some kind of sense. Okay. But if his suit comes out the way he wants, the agency gets the exclusive on the parklands addition, which is very fat. I certainly am not going to let go of it. If we get it, I'm responsible for getting it. You can't buy me out of that."

"If I owned this agency, I don't think I'd get that close to Loomis."

"What's eight percent of fifty mil?"

"Lots of money. Remember, if the agency has an exclusive on the Parklands addition, that potential return will have to be figured into the appraisal of the total value of the corporation. You better go get your hand looked at. I don't think there's anything more we can talk about now. I've got a couple of things to do. I'll lock up. Can you drive?"

"I can drive." Bern picked his jacket up off the couch and went to the open door of his office, stopped there and turned and looked back at Wade. It aws an odd moment, a condensation of the years, a twisting of time. He shook his head, shrugged and walked out.

Wade waited a few minutes before leaving Bern's office. He fingered the tender spot over his ear. Fourteen years should end with more drama. Flintlock pistols, seconds in black capes, a measured count, turn and fire. Or swordplay in the castle keep, with the dames in lace watching.

And the parting should be caused by something more honorable than getting caught up in the footwork of a skilled swindler.

8

Helen Yoder took the Morans to two houses she was reasonably certain they would not like so that the third one would look that much more attractive to them. The Willoughby house was twenty years old, a three-bedroom two-bath on Garden Street, a dead-end street six blocks from the waterfront. It was well placed on a nice wooded lot.

A retired couple had bought it when it was first constructed, and the survivor had died there, alone, six months ago. The house and grounds had not been properly maintained. Essentially, the house was sound. She had gone over it with Fred Aird, the senior trust officer at the West Bay Citizens Bank. They were old friends and had worked together on many projects. She said it would be tough to move it as is for, say, ninety thousand. But if they would put in ten thousand, a horseback guess, then she thought she could move it for a hundred and twenty.

Fred had agreed, and so the kitchen was shining new, the roof repainted white, interior trim touched up, carpeting cleaned, draperies repaired and the grounds trimmed and landscaped, holes in the driveway patched.

Thomas and Alyce Moran were a newly retired couple from Cedar Rapids. They didn't get to the Willoughby house until after eleven. By that time she had established a useful relationship with them. She had learned to be on the watch for all the cues. With some of the prospects, if you were even borderline flirtatious with the husband, you killed any possible sale. Some wanted to keep a cold distance from the salesperson. Others wanted instant warm buddyship. She ascertained her role with the Morans and fitted herself into it. She and the wife were on one side, appreciative of the needs and the labors of the housewife. And so they both catered to the lordly whims and opinions of Thomas Moran, knowing well that Alyce would make the final decision.

It was a lovely September morning, with the clarity that mornings used to have along the Gulf Coast. And that helped the sale. The two women let Tom believe he was making the decision. When he feigned reluctance and questioned the price, Helen said she might be able to get it for a hundred and eighteen five. And so then they went to lunch where Helen phoned Fred and asked him how he liked eighteen five, and Fred told her she was a genius and she told him they were both geniuses, so she told the Morans the deal was on and it turned into a celebration lunch which Mr. Moran insisted on buying. And then they went to the bank, signed papers, presented a check to go into escrow, worked out the mortgage terms and arranged a date and time for the closing at the Mississippi Title Insurance Company.

Helen was back in the office by three-fifteen. She saw through the open door that Bern was in his office alone, so she went to his doorway and said, "Hey, we just sold the Willoughby house."

"Great," he said flatly. "Come on in and close the door and sit down."

"Well yes *sir*, Colonel sir!"

"Sorry, Helen. I apologize. I'm kind of distracted. I wanted to give you some advance news. Some early news that you have to keep to yourself. Okay?"

"Well sure."

"We're going to split up, Wade and me. One of us is going to get to keep the corporation, but we don't know which one yet. Let's say it's a personality conflict."

"I'm sorry it has to happen. I really am. But it . . . it isn't a great big fat surprise exactly. I mean things haven't been a lot of laughs around here lately."

"It's fair to tell you that I think I'll wind up with the agency. I have some very promising negotiations going on right now with Tuck Loomis. Helen, I have a lot of respect for your ability in this field. You're the only one I've talked to. I would certainly feel a lot better about this split if I knew you would stay with me, with the company. I'm sorry we had that little problem in the past."

"It's forgotten."

"No, it isn't forgotten. I was a damn fool. I wouldn't have come on to you like that if I hadn't had one or two drinks too many. And I forgot you were married to Buddy at the time."

"I still am."

"I mean you were still living with him. Anyway, it was a bad move on my part, and I'm sorry it happened. It made a lot of awkwardness. I just want you to know that it won't ever happen again. I don't know why it ever happened in the first place."

"Neither do I. God knows I'm no debutante. I don't ask for problems but they keep happening. I guess in a way it's flattering. But it can be a damned nuisance."

"I want to say I appreciate you not telling Nita."

"Why should I? She's a friend. And it isn't like you got anywhere near first base. I never told anybody, Bern. I don't have so many women friends I can afford to waste one. Matter of fact I don't have hardly any."

"I think that when I have this agency—after the Bernard Island thing is settled—Tuck Loomis and I are going to have a very long and profitable relationship. And you fit into the picture of the agency the way I want it to be."

"Will Wade be opening his own agency?"

"If I end up with this one, I guess he will. There's nothing in our aggreements to prevent either of us from opening up a new place after a buyout."

"Thanks for letting me know, and—"

"You don't have to make a decision right now. It's

an important step. Just think it over carefully, Helen. That's all I ask. And I might say that if you decide to stay with me—providing I buy Wade out, of course—we'll review your commission arrangements with an eye to making things a little sweeter for you."

She stood up. "Okay, Bern. I'll keep thinking about it."

"Please don't tell anyone about this little talk."

"You know I won't."

After she had given Jeanie Nash the documents and data to record the sale in the master file, along with the check for escrow, she went to her bull-pen desk and went through her mail, dropping most of it into the wastebasket. She sat frowning into space, then phoned the law firm of Fetts, Kimball, Loudner and O'Rourke and asked for Mr. Hubbard Yoder. The switchboard connected her with Buddy's secretary. "And who shall I say is calling?"

"Mrs. Yoder."

"Just a moment, please."

It was a long moment. Buddy always needed time to think about what he was going to say next. He had a big handsome weathered face, a long jaw, crisp wavy black hair with a curl that hung down on his forehead. He had smile wrinkles, and a charming white-toothed grin. He had great shoulders and a deep chest, narrow waist and short thick bowed legs. Seated at a table with other people, he looked like a big tall man. When he stood up he was so close to her height, she was careful about wearing high heels. He was a very nice man. People liked him. He was a junior partner at the firm. He made good money. He was tidy and generous and drank sparingly. He loved her dearly, and she couldn't imagine why she had married him almost four years ago.

He had a slow methodical uncomplicated mind. He had not the slightest trace of a sense of humor. He laughed readily, but it was merely audible cheefulness. He talked easily about baseball, basketball, football, fishing, golf, tennis, swimming and sailing. His opinions were subject to immediate change when anyone disagreed with him. Of the sports he talked about, golf and fishing were the only ones he attempted. He was bad at both because he had very little physical coordination. He slept eight hours a night and exercised for a half hour before his shower every morning. In bed he seemed to have no limberness or flexibility. His body was board-like, his caresses predictable, his climax forever the same.

In the beginning when she had discovered the humorlessness, she began to invent pointless little jokes. She would tell him and they would laugh together and she would feel ashamed of herself.

After she had at last realized, a year or so into the marriage, that he was the most boring person she had ever known, she began to wonder how she could get out of it. He was faithful and he adored her. He kept telling her he hoped she would get pregnant. That thought made her heart sink because it meant a lifetime of Buddy Yoder.

At last she decided there was no reason that boredom could not be considered a sufficient cause. He didn't want her to work. He said he was making enough money. She knew she would go screaming

131

crazy out of her mind if the only things in her day were the condo apartment and lunch with friends and all the rest of the time with Buddy Yoder.

Finally, two months ago, she'd told him to move out. He could not understand it. She helped him pack. He kept wanting to leave things behind. She wouldn't let him. He went to live with his sister and her husband. They had a little guest house in the backyard. He was still confused about it. He kept asking her if there was someone else, and when she said no, he would ask her who it was. After he moved out, it was as if she had cracked a cocoon and emerged—a cocoon made of seventy pounds of damp putty. Her life had come back to life.

"Well, hey Helen! How you, honeybun?"

"Just great, Buddy. Couldn't be better. Did Dan Patrick get in touch with you?"

"Well, yes. Yes he did. And I told Dan we just needed a little time to work things out between us."

"Now look. That's just crap, Buddy. Dan is representing me and I am paying him to work out a no-fault divorce. Okay? I don't want anything at all. I've got some income from Cordell's estate and I've got what I make here. I just sold a house today. I'm going to sell the condo and send you the money. Or, if you want, I can find myself a place and you can move back in. What do you want?"

"I just don't understand all this. I tried every way I know how to make you happy, honeybun. I just don't understand it. It's the worst thing that... that ever... ever happened to me."

She realized he was crying again. She took a deep

breath and let it out in a long sigh. "Oh shit, Buddy. Cut it out. I want to get this thing settled."

"Will you do me one favor?"

"What's the catch?"

"If you do me this one favor, then I'll go along with anything you want."

"What's the favor?"

"You just put this whole divorce idea out of your mind for six months. Just don't think about it at all. And then you won't get so anxious about doing it in such a big hurry."

She thought it over. "I have your word?"

"You sure do, honeybun."

"Okay, on one condition. Stop hassling me for those six months, Buddy. No flowers, no loving telegrams, no phone calls. And stop putting that money in my account every month."

"I want you to have the money."

"But I don't *want* it. I don't *need* it. I don't want to *take* it!"

"Well . . . could I take you out to dinner once a month?"

"No."

"How about I take you out to dinner in the middle of the six months, like three months from today. That would make it the third of December. Just so we can find out how . . . we're getting along."

She sighed again. "Okay, okay, okay."

"Suppose we run into each other like on the street or at a party or something. Can we say hello, how are you, that stuff?"

"Yes we can. But we are not going to make a special effort to run into each other, are we?"

"I guess not. No. I won't do that. Will you tell Dan to come back in six months?"

"Yes, I will."

"Maybe he won't have to come back at all. Maybe by then you'll get over this idea."

"Buddy, what I've got isn't a head cold or a limp."

"If you'd only tell me *why*."

"I told you. I just don't want to be married anymore. To anybody."

She heard him sigh. It sounded a little bit ragged. "How are things going otherwise?" he asked.

"Pretty good. But I think Wade and Bern are going to split up. I'm not supposed to be telling this to anyone. It won't be until after the Bernard Island suit is settled. I hear you're in on that."

"Yes I am," he said, new life in his voice. "Me and Bobby Tom. It's been all set for the eleventh, Thursday, a week from tomorrow. We've got some kind of visuals we're taking over there. We'll have two vanloads of stuff. And you wouldn't believe the documentation. And we've got some real impressive appraisers to take the stand."

"Do you think you'll have an easy win?"

"We've had these conferences with Tuck Loomis and his people. We've got to show the Court that they could really have gotten all their ducks in a row and developed that island and they could have turned it into something great, something that would be a showcase for the whole Mississippi coast. All they have to do is show that it would be a damn poor place to build on. I just feel it might be easier to be on the other side of this case. But we're getting all geared up."

"Buddy, you keep your guard up, hear? Just be careful what goes on around you. You are a good honest man and people can use you."

"What's that supposed to mean?"

"You know I went with Tuck before I married you."

"Yes, I know. And I can't understand how you could let a man old enough to be your—"

"We went through that years ago. Now hush up. There isn't anything I can tell you except that Tucker Loomis has never in his life gone into any kind of a fight without he has an edge. He works things out in advance so that they come out his way every time. He laughs a lot. I just mean if you see anything going on you think is wrong, you get out. Tell them you've got the flu. Go to bed for a week."

After a silence he said, "Helen, if I am such a good honest man, how come you don't want to be married to me anymore?"

"That has nothing to do with it."

"You're going to drive me . . . complete out of—"

"Don't you start crying again, dammit! Say goodbye."

"Goodbye, honeybun."

"Goodbye to you, Buddy."

Wade had a junk-food lunch a few blocks from the office on Thursday at noon, and when it was time to return he went to a pay phone and called Ellie Service and told her that something had come up and he wouldn't be able to get back to the office. He could not remember lying to her before for no reason at all. She reminded him of an appointment and he told her to switch it to Friday or Monday, whatever.

Beth's Toyota was in the carport when he drove in and Tod's ten-speed was there too, locked to the ring he had screwed to the wall. Summer school had ended and the regular session would begin on Monday. When he walked in through the kitchen he could hear the muted thump of the music from Tod's room. The kid spent a lot of nice afternoons indoors lately.

Beth had changed to a blue halter and shorts and she was at the living-room desk bringing her sales records up-to-date, biting her lip, glasses halfway down her nose, hair tousled.

She took her glasses off and turned and looked at him, eyebrows raised in question. "Have you left the agency already, dear?"

"Hey, come *on*."

"It's a legitimate question. I think I have a right to know. I mean I wasn't allowed any input on whether or not you should decide to break up with Bern. I'd just like to know when it happens."

"It's doesn't happen like this when it happens. There'll be conferences with the lawyers and negotiations and all kinds of crap."

"But once the decision is made, what's the point of hanging around? If something is over it's over, isn't it?"

"As yet we don't know who'll get the agency."

"What in the world is going to keep Bern from getting it?"

He sat on the far side of the room. "I wouldn't

136

know. I told you last night we aren't going to discuss it until the Bernard Island thing is over. And that's on the docket for a week from today at ten in the morning."

"Don't use that tired draggy voice when you talk about it to me, Wade. This is my life too. I'm not some chattel."

"What I tried to tell you last night, and you wouldn't listen, is that this has been coming on for a long time, this split. Tuck's scam is what lit the fuse. If it hadn't been Bernard Island it would have been something else."

"Maybe it was what you did. Maybe you . . . incited it. Ever think of that?"

"Will you listen?"

"Of course! Go right ahead."

"I did not like Bern's getting us tied up with Tuck Loomis in the way it was done. It made us a part of his conspiracy to defraud. Bern wouldn't listen to my bitching. He wanted easy money and we got it. So when I found out that some of the deeds were improper, I made contact with Hammond from the Park Service and gave him the information. He said he would pass it along to the U.S. Attorney's Office. Somebody in that office evidently passed the information back to Loomis. He chewed Bern out and gave orders to delete those four deeds from our records, and he even got the records at the court house changed. I would imagine that's a crime, but I don't know what to call it. Bern thinks I've conspired against him."

"Haven't you?"

"A squall comes up and your engine quits and you start drifting into trouble. So you throw out a sea anchor and it hauls your bow around into the wind and you ride it out. I smelled trouble. I threw out a sea anchor. If they ever impanel a grand jury to dig into this whole mess, Gordon Hammond is going to be able to testify as to exactly what I did and what I said, and what he did with my information."

"Does that make you a noble person or a sneak?"

"Why are we doing this? What's the point? It doesn't make me *into* anything. I do what I do because I am what I am."

"Popeye the Sailor Man."

He got up and walked over to her and put his hand on her shoulder. She wrenched forward, away from his touch. "If you've stopped liking what I am," he said gently, "we have some big problems. I like what you are, how you think, what you do. I love you. It's a good thing to like the person you love."

She came up out of the chair, turning as she did so, quickly sliding up into his arms. She buried her face in his shoulder and trembled against him, making an odd sound, not a sob or a sigh. Something in between.

"I get scared," she said. "You know."

And he did know. Any threat of insecurity was deadly. She had lived in a golden world until she was eight, a little girl loved and treasured and admired. A beautiful little girl in a beautiful home, wearing beautiful clothes. And suddenly the sky went dark. As it does in the stories of witches and goblins. The mother dwindled and sickened and shrank and died, as if under a spell. The father changed jobs, changed to one where he traveled all over the world. The cherished girl was sent to live with her aunt and uncle who had five loud rowdy children of their own in a house too small. There she learned to keep herself to herself, to fend off aggression, to keep her face closed, her head down, and do as she was told. And he knew that he could never build for her a world so fine but that she would always be waiting for the first hint the sky was growing dark. She had learned long ago that nothing lasted, and had learned the lesson all too well.

"Either way, Beth honey, everything will be fine. Either way. We'll make out."

"Sure. I know. Don't mind me." She turned away, out of his arms, and with her back to him said, "You had lunch?"

"Yes, thanks. I think I'd like to take the Whaler and go on out, maybe to Horn Island. Want to come along? It's a beautiful day."

"I've got to finish the August report and mail it in. Why don't you take Tod?"

"If he'll come. The last two times I asked him he didn't want to go."

"Make him go with you. He spends too much time in his room lately."

She turned and smiled at him, the smile self-mocking.

"You okay now?" he asked.

"I'm fine. Just don't mind too much if I snarl at you sometimes. Okay?"

"I don't mind at all."

It took twenty-five minutes to run from the West Bay Marina out to the beach just west of the big lagoon on

Horn Island. There was barely enough breeze to kick up a small chop out of the southwest. Every once in a while the bow would lift and smack down, whacking the white spray out to either side. He stood at the console, knees slightly bent. Tod sat forward on the port side. Wade could see the gentle curve of his cheek, line of jaw, shadow of eyelashes. Heritage from Beth. It was strange to see this dwindling girlishness, this essence of vulnerability, and know that in another year or two the last of it would be gone and the man would have taken its place, all planes and angles and leathery knots. And no matter how fiercely denied, that feminine factor would still be inside, buried but vulnerable.

They tilted the mtor up and pulled the Whaler onto the shallow beach west of the lagoon.

"What are we going to do now?" Tod asked in a tired and patient voice.

"Walk in the woods. Show you something."

No response. The boy followed him through the woods of pine and oak and scrub palmetto, and up the long slope of a dune. Wade stopped at the crest of the dune and said, "Not ready yet."

"What's not ready."

Wade indicated the four or five brushy acres that stretched out below them, toward the sea beach on the far side of the island. "Soon that whole open patch will be all bright yellow flowers. It's worth seeing. We can come out again."

"Don't bother on my account."

Wade grinned at him. "You too macho to look at flowers?"

"Whatever."

Wade walked over to a log and said, "Come on over here and sit."

The boy did as he was told, and lifted his shoulders in a long sigh of patience and the expectation of a lecture.

"Tod, your mother and I have been wondering and worrying a little bit about you. You seem kind of down lately."

"What is that supposed to mean? Down."

"Down means down. Gloomy, depressed, troubled. This would be a good time to talk about it, don't you think?"

"I don't know what there is to talk about."

"Look, we're proud of you. We think you are what is uncommonly known as a good kid. If something is bothering you, then it is bothering us too."

Tod's stare was flat. "Whatever could it be?" The tone was a half degree away from insolence.

"Can I ask questions then?"

"Whatever."

"I don't mean to pry. I remember that sixteen is kind of a rotten time of life. Sixteen to eighteen. Then it gets a little better. So you are into the first year of the three years when life can be totally the shits from time to time."

He saw that he had startled the boy. "For everybody?" he asked.

"I don't know how it is for everybody. I have the feeling that the more thoughtful a person is, maybe the more sensitive and the more curious, the rougher time he'll have. There are some people who live their whole life in a vegetable state. They don't read. They don't think. They don't care. They're like some lower form of life in a lab. Jab them and they'll flinch, and that's the way you know they're even alive. They did that intelligence testing last year, so we know you are brighter than the average, Tod."

"I don't feel bright."

"It kind of surprised your mother and me when you messed up and had to take these summer-school courses."

"The grades will be okay."

"I'm glad you did it. It will save time later, maybe a whole year. Does it make you feel good to know you did well?"

The boy shrugged. "I don't know. It doesn't seem to mean a hell of a lot one way or another, you know."

"Too many kids get bogged down in problems that seem a lot more important than they really are. And they drop out. That's a dead end."

"Maybe."

"Being sixteen doesn't mean the problem can't be man-size. I am not patronizing you. But there is one ground rule. That's what parents are supposed to do. Make the rules. Here is the rule. You have been in the dumps for about a week. If in another two weeks you are not back to normal, or, I should say, back to what we are used to, then we go find a counselor for you. And you can unload on him or her whatever it is you can't or won't confide in us. Is that a fair deal?"

"I don't have any choice?"

"I just told you you have three choices. Back to

norm. Or lay it on our doorstep. Or we find help for you."

"That doesn't sound like much of a choice."

"If nobody makes the rules then it turns into a game without any rules, and nobody wins that kind of a game."

"Are you looking to win something?"

"I'm looking not to lose something. We don't want to force you into being a certain kind of person. Do you understand that? My son, the doctor. My son, the lawyer. My son, the astronaut. What we want for you and Kim is for each of you to fulfill your own potential in your own way. We're around to see that while you are kind of feeling your way into life, you don't screw your life up on account of something that seems terribly important right now, but isn't."

"Dad, how can *you* know what's important these days?"

"Probably the same exact things that were important when my great-grandfather was a kid. The big things. Honor and faith and justice and love. And pride. That belongs in there. Pride in yourself. Don't duck away from the big words just because they sound too straight."

"Things are different than they were in the olden days."

"Underneath, things are always the same. On top, on the surface, all the fads and fancies and quote new ideas end quote are just a lot of random noise."

"If you say so."

"Think it out for yourself, Tod. The big words still work."

143

"Okay."

"Do we have a deal?"

"I guess so. Okay." The boy looked sidelong at him and got up from his position straddling the log. He bent and picked a sand spur off the side of his gray running shoe. He looked at Wade again and then walked over to the crest and looked out across the brushy meadowland. He had looked at his father with curiosity combined with a small astonishment. You have to keep showing them a little more of yourself each year that goes by, Wade thought, or you become a stick figure, a drawing of daddy, a kind of symbol of outgrown authority. And if you stay too far away from their sulks and despairs, you can end up like Bruce and Jean Addison wondering for the rest of their lives why they hadn't given Karen some help before she hung herself.

"All yellow flowers, eh?" Tod asked.

"Yellow and gold. Thick with them. A big bright blanket."

"Next month?"

"I'd say a couple or three weeks. There's some just beginning to show over there on the far left."

"It must be something to see."

"If I get tied up at work or anything, take the Whaler and come out for a look. Bring a friend. And bring a sieve and a bucket. You can get some nice coquinas on the outside beach as it gets cooler."

"I know."

"Would you like to go take a look at Bernard Island? I can show you how Loomis claims he was going to subdivide it."

"Why not?" the boy said listlessly. But, watching and listening carefully, Wade decided that the listlessness was not quite as genuine as it had been. Tod had adopted an attitude toward this little excursion today, and he was not about to abandon it all of a sudden no matter how he might feel about it. So it was a question of honor and of consistency. Wade had the belief he had pried open a small window and let in some light that sooner or later would become welcome.

 9

Early on a lazy Sunday afternoon Tuck and Maria were entangled in another one of Maria's experiments. She was unrelentingly inventive, and as intent, ritualistic and consumed as a child with a new dollhouse. The bedroom draperies were closed, leaving his room in a golden half-light. It diminished the contrast between their bodies, his crenelated skin, gray body hair, sagging brawn and her slender ivory elegance. He told himself he did not hear the door chimes. He told himself he had merely imagined them. At last Maria said in a rusty voice tight with strain, "Maybe they'll go away. Oh God, make them go away. Please."

He cursed, pulled away from her despite her groan of protest, donned his yellow terrycloth robe and padded to the front door. He saw that it was his dockmaster, Jack Simms, standing out there, reaching with his thumb to sound the chimes again. He opened the door and said, "For chrissake, Jack!"

"Jeez, I wake you up, Mr. Loomis? Hey, I'm sorry. I saw both your cars and I figured you were in."

"What do you want?"

"I don't know if it's important or not. It's about somebody talking to Ez Feeney about those deeds we're supposed to forget about we ever signed them."

His irritation faded. "That's the gate guard, the tall skinny one?"

"Yes sir."

"Come on in, Jack." He took him to a corner of the big living room where a long couch and two chairs and a coffee table were placed to facilitate private conversations. Simms dusted the seat of his cutoffs with both hands before sitting cautiously on the couch.

"Who is talking to Feeney?"

"Well, not anymore. I mean it was back a ways, this man came to see him and said he was from the real estate people, Rowley/Gibbs. He faked Feeney out. Fed him some shit about how he could maybe get ten thousand dollars from the feds for having give up his land out on the island. Feeney told him that I couldn't afford that kind of land either. He gave Feeney his business card, and his name is Wade Rowley."

"I'm a lot closer to his partner, Bern Gibbs. We figured out it was Rowley tried to shove a stick in our wheels. Look, I didn't mean to come down so hard on you boys. I was mad as hell. There's a lot at stake here. It wasn't your fault I had you sign those papers. I just want you and Feeney to forget it. Okay?"

"What I came to ask you about, Mr. Loomis, this

147

Feeney he keeps after me. He's not exactly a hot head, you know. But he don't like anybody jerking him around like this Rowley did."

"So?"

"He keeps after me he should call the number on the card and ask this Rowley to come back to Feeney's trailer, he wants to tell him something. Feeney wants that I should be there and the two of us we should bump him around some. Feeney says it would teach him a lesson. I don't know if it's such a great idea and I told Feeney I'd see what you think, whether it would mess up anything for you."

The images of Maria in heat kept sliding into the edge of his mind, mouth torn sideways, eyes swooning, belly sleek with sweat.

"I don't know," he said. "Well, why not? But not with Feeney. I don't want him there even. He starts yakking and there's no damn way in the world to shut him up. What you do, Jack, you take Mike Wasser with you. Set it up when Feeney's working the gate so you can use his old white pickup. Don't mention any names at all to Rowley. Just tell him he should keep his nose out of other folks' business. Don't do a hospital job on him and don't break up his face. Bust up his middle and knock him down and kick his ass blue." He stood up and Simms stood up on cue, and as Simms followed him to the door he said, "You got any questions?"

"I'm wondering what to tell Feeney."

"Work it out yourself. I don't want him in on it."

"When should we do it?"

"We go to court on Thursday. Better do it before

then. They may have the son of a bitch set up to testify. Maybe he'll forget what he was going to tell them."

As soon as the front door was closed and locked, Tuck hurried back to Maria. As he came through the door, dropping the robe on the floor behind him, she hopped off the bed and positioned herself as before on the big square leather hassock they had moved into his bedroom from the living room. He grinned at her and knelt between her knees.

After they were back on the king-size bed he dozed for a time and then came awake with a start and saw that it was almost three-thirty. He poked her awake. She lifted a sleepmazed frowning face and said, "Wha's up?"

"You got a lot to do before Shirley gets here to relieve you."

She grabbed his wrist and turned it to see his watch. Hers was pinned to her uniform. "Sangre de Cristo!" she said and hopped out of bed and headed in a hurry toward the bathroom. Watching her he marveled that her behind looked bigger and rounder when it was bare than when it was under the white fabric of her uniform.

Something was making him uncomfortable and soon he realized he was uneasy about Jack Simms' visit. Feeney's idea wasn't a very good idea. The more he thought about it, the stupider it seemed. Too damn anxious to get back to the interrupted piece of ass. Agree to anything in that condition. Lose his head, like the little dog on the railroad tracks. He backed up and thought it through. What could happen? If Row-

John D. MacDonald

ley wanted to make a big case about it, nobody would
know what the hell he was talking about. Maybe Rowley reached for the wrong woman and the husband or
boyfriend kicked the living shit out of him, and he was
trying to make it sound like something else entirely.

He knew he should get up and go find Jack Simms
in the marina area and call it off. Muscle stuff is pointless, especially when there are so many more satisfying
ways to make a man sorry he's alive. He yawned and
stretched and yawned again, thinking about getting up.

While Maria dressed she glanced over at Tuck from
time to time. He was on his back, snoring slowly and
regularly, the big thatched chest lifting and falling, his
mouth hanging open. She floated a wool afghan over
him. He stirred as it settled upon him but did not
awaken. Being with him was an excitement she had
never experienced before. She remembered having felt
something akin to it when she was little and they had
taken the kids to the zoo one day. She had stayed behind the others at the lion stockade. They had come
back and gotten her and scolded her. She had been
staring into the great somber eyes of the nearest lion.
She had wanted to be closer to him. She had wanted to
touch him.

Tuck was not a wild beast, but he was a hard and
dangerous man with a ruthlessness she feared and re-
spected, and an improbable amount of money. They
had been making love for seven weeks, on weekend
afternoons and often in the morning before Lottie and
Henry came to work. She had never suspected that a
man of his years would have such powerful physical
needs. She had very slowly and carefully seduced him

150

into acts which, in the beginning, he had not wanted to attempt, thinking perhaps that they were unsuitable to a man of his stature and importance. When she went too far too quickly, she annoyed him and that made him rough and quick with her, as he had been in the very beginning. Wham-bam-thank-you-ma'am. But now he was doing whatever she asked of him, and she had taught him to think about and respect her pleasure before taking his own. He was such an apt student she found herself approaching a peak of sexuality she had seldom reached before, an immediate readiness, orgasms so prolonged they became a variety of agony. And her heightened sensory awareness in turn enlarged and extended his. It was as if she were taming something, teaching and controlling and using it, knowing all the time she was on dangerous ground, but wanting to take additional chances each time, feeling a growing flavor of affection for the old man. It was a totally physical infatuation, an immersion in the rolling, gasping flesh, and she knew it had to end but right now she did not want to think about when or how.

She looked at her watch. Ten of four. She rechecked her hair and makeup in the bathroom mirror, and closed the bedroom door quietly as she left his room. She hurried to Mrs. Loomis' room and found her asleep. With a quick light touch she straightened the blanket without awakening her. The afternoon sun was moving closer to the bed. She adjusted the blinds, and in a few moments she heard Shirley drive in. She went to the back door and unlocked and opened it for her.

"How are things?" Shirley asked.

"Madame is asleep. And so is the head man. The

phones are turned off. She had a little fever this morning, sub-normal at noon."

"Thanks. I'll want the phone on, at least until nine. My son is going to phone here from Miami."

"Well, I'm off."

"Take care. See you tomorrow, love."

As Maria drove out of Parklands, through the gate and down to the Arden River Road, she was feeling guilty about not wrestling Thelma Loomis out of her bed and into the wheelchair for a little ride around the grounds after lunch. But there was no way Thelma could snitch. Blame it on the little fever she had ran. And not on my little fever, she thought. As she approached West Bay she was stopped by a red light. When the light changed she tried to accelerate and stalled. Damn old anitque Ford Falcon. Junk. She tried three times before it caught. It ran the battery down, and had it not caught on that third attempt, she would have been really hung up.

The two of them back there in that eight-hundred-thousand-dollar house, sound asleep. Two cars worth maybe sixty thousand total sitting there in the big carport. What if? What if? Ah, what a world it would become! First-class air travel. Cruises. Darling clothes. Could that tough old son of a bitch be wheedled into marrying a second-generation Mexican nurse thirty years younger than he? Can Maria find happiness in a *Dallas* setting? What do bears do in the woods?

One would have to move just as slowly and carefully and cleverly as during the past seven weeks. And if the affair peaked and then began to fade, and *then* the old lady died, the answer is no. Maria is fun and games, but not a wife. But if he is hanging on the edge and it happens, then...possibly. 'My darling, you have to get away from all this for a while. Let Maria help you, dear. What we both need is a fun place to take our minds off all this. Yes, she was a dear sweet woman and I know you'll miss her.'

Make a mental note. The sons and their wives and the grandchildren will come to the services. And you will be that little dark-haired nurse who was so awfully fond of old Thelma. Give them no clue at all. Cry a lot.

'Hey, Tuck, let's sneak off to a fun place all by ourselves. Like maybe Vegas? Just for a week or two, hon. To help you get over this terrible loss.' And then, in Vegas, a little fun and frolic and booze and a sudden girlish reluctance to make love with a newly bereaved husband. A few days of that and then one day lots of drinks and then, just for sport, just for laughs, we'll get married in one of those tacky little chapels. How do you know how soon you might *need* a nurse just for nursing, old man?

But the old lady. That was the problem. She would never be able to walk or talk again. She could hang in there for thirty more years. Unless steps are taken. Soon. Very very careful steps. Easing someone over the edge, a person that is more thing than person, is actually doing the old biddy a favor. The look in her eyes tells you she is having a bad time of it, that she hates it. Even if she goes, maybe Tuck is too tough and smart to be suckered into marriage again so soon. Maybe. That comes to a question of risk. Is it worth the chance to do it and come up empty? Depends on the chance of getting caught. Review the status of the patient. Diminished kidney function, slight congestive heart failure problem, low blood pressure. So go home and read the medications book and check off everything contraindicated, and then go into the box in the back of the closet and see if there's anything there that might, in itself, be sufficiently bad for her, or maybe sufficiently bad if substituted for the medications she's now taking. No seizures. Just gently gently down the tube, fading sweetly away into forever. No autopsy, thank you. And if, through medication, she dies of what's already wrong with her, who's to worry?

No! I'm just kidding around. Just playing mental games. Just playing pretend. I'm not that sort of person. I'm a *nurse*. There is a code of medical ethics. Just like the doctors, we give no deadly drug. But, of course, if it should work out, then I wouldn't be a nurse anymore, would I? And I wouldn't have to think about a lot of rules.

At twelve-twenty on Tuesday, the ninth of September, the only two people in the Rowley/Gibbs offices were Jeanie Nash up front and Dawn Marino back at her desk outside Bern's big office. Dawn was doing her nails and tapping her foot to the muted music on her little green radio, an old country favorite by Willy.

When her phone rang she picked up the receiver with one hand and turned off the music with the other. Jeanie said, "I got a guy on another line hot to talk to Wade. He's called back a couple of times. He won't say what he wants. Do you want to give it a try?"

"Why not?"

"Lots of luck. Here he is."

"Mr. Rowley's secretary," she said sweetly.

"Well, I wanted to talk to him."

"I don't know when he'll be back, really. Maybe I can help."

"Okay. Maybe you can. But I got to know if he'll be able to keep an appointment at four o'clock today."

"Does he know about the appointment?"

"No. I'm making it now, okay?"

"Let me look at his schedule."

"Sure."

She stared into space for a little while and then said, "He should be free at four o'clock."

"You going to write this down?"

"I have already written it down, sir."

"Tell him to be at Feeney's place at four. Tell him Feeney has some more things he ought to know."

"How do you spell Feeney?"

"How the hell many ways can there be? You just tell him. Okay?"

"Yes, I'll—" But the man hung up.

Jeanie had walked back to Dawn's desk. "Okay?"

Dawn smiled at her and looked beyond her. "All taken care of, dear. I think my boss has come to take me to lunch."

"How nice for you!"

"Isn't it, though?"

The Waveland Motel was ten miles west of West Bay on Route 90. Bern Gibbs swung in and parked his dark blue BMW around in the back and then walked to the front office for the key. Garcia was on the desk. He

155

nodded and picked the key off the rack and slapped it down in front of Bern.

"Don't you give me that smirk, boy, or I'll get Stace to fire your ass out of here."

"Big deal. Who would he get to work as cheap as me? Maybe I'll quit anyways. This little old place is next thing to dead."

As he walked back to the unit he wondered if it made any sense to keep on sneaking out here to be with Dawn. If Tuck knew about it, a lot of other people knew about it. And sooner or later Nita would know about it. He didn't like to think of what that might do to her. But he couldn't think of any way he could stop himself from doing what he was doing. The small pale body of Dawn Marino was addictive. Strange, because she was constructed so much like Nita. The same disproportionately heavy thighs, same slight overbite, same large black pubic V, same large brown aureoles around her nipples. But this body was magic and the other one had become boring.

He unlocked the door and they went in and turned on the rackety air conditioner. They undressed in haste and piled onto the bed and, within moments were joined, thrusting, moaning. After they had sagged into postcoital surfeit, they moved to lie side by side, her left leg heavy across his lower belly.

"God, I needed you," she said. "I kept thinking about it all morning."

"Me too."

"Just before you got to the office a funny thing happened."

"What kind of funny?"

"Funny like strange. There was this call for Wade and the man told Jeanie it was important. Both Ellie and Wade were out and she couldn't get rid of the guy so she gave me the call and I let him think I was Wade's secretary. He set up an appointment for Wade to meet him at Feeney's place at four this afternoon. He said Feeney had something to tell him."

"Does Jeanie know what he wanted?"

"No, I didn't tell her. I just told her I took care of it. What is Feeney's place? Like a bar?"

"Did the man tell Jeanie what he wanted before he told you?"

"No. And I didn't leave any message for Wade either."

The rackety window air conditioner cycled again, starting with a thump, settling down to a rumble. As he looked at her she stuck her lower lip out and blew her dark hair away from her eye, and smiled at him.

"So the man thinks Wade will be there?"

"I guess so."

"He didn't give a name?"

"No."

"What did he sound like?"

"What do you mean?"

"Like an educated man or a bum or what?"

"He sounded like anybody. It was just a voice. Maybe a little bit rough-sounding. You know, like he would have a temper. Like he wouldn't put up with any kind of shit."

"Maybe I'll keep the appointment."

"Maybe that isn't real smart, lover."

"Wade has been sneaking around behind my back trying to screw up my relationship with Tuck."

"I know. I think it's rotten. After all you've done for him. You bring in most of the business. He acts half asleep most of the time. I can't understand how come the other people think he's so great."

"This sounds like some more conspiracy against me and Tuck. My God, they go to court this Thursday. Maybe if I go, I can keep something else from going wrong."

"Wade will find out."

"Afterwards."

"I think it would make him pretty sore, you keeping one of his appointments, honey. If you can find out where it is."

"Not as sore as he made me. I nearly broke my hand on his thick skull. I still can hardly move this thumb."

"Well, you do what you think is best."

"I wonder who will be at Feeney's place."

"But where is it?"

"That's Ezra Feeney, dear. One of the four names you erased off the computer list. There was a home address."

"Oh."

"I've got the address at the office. I'll scout it out early."

"Bern?"

"Yes, sweet girl?"

"Have you given it any thought, I mean about when you're going to tell Nita about us?"

"Yes, I have given it some thought."

"Well?"

"I keep worrying about Lois. It creates a lot of emotional trauma for a kid when the parents split up. What I want to do is lessen the impact on her. You understand?"

"It's not like she's some little kid! She's seventeen, Bern."

"And she'll be eighteen in December, yes. But she's not one of those brash kids. She's not tough. She'd really be very vulnerable to anything like this. She's very close to both of us."

"Is it doing her any good to be in a house where there's no love and laughter?"

"You've got a point. But look at it this way. Next September she'll be going off to school. There'll be a lot of new impressions flooding in on her. A lot of things to keep her mind busy. In a sense she'll really be leaving home."

"Next *September*!"

"That isn't so far away. It's just one year, honey."

She pushed herself away from him, rolled, swung her legs off the bed and got up. She walked to the window, held the draperies open a few inches and looked out at Bern's car and at the mound of trash under the trees beyond the parking area. She spun and glared at him.

"A whole *year*!"

"You'll be surprised how fast it will go by, Dawn. Look, we'll be together every working day. And we can be together like this whenever we have a chance. You're so beautiful, darling. I don't know what I ever did to deserve having you."

159

"A whole *year*!"

"Wait a minute! I thought we were talking abot the rest of our lives together. Do you want us to start off on a sour note?"

"Of course not, but . . ."

"I might be depressed for a long time if out of pure selfishness we screwed up my little daughter's life."

"Eighteen in December! For God's sake, I'm only twenty-three!"

"It would be a terrible shock for her right now."

"You know what, Bern? If I'm going to have to wait a whole year, so are you." She came back and sat on the edge of the bed.

"What do you mean by that?"

"Absolutely no more ass at all until we get married. And I mean it. You have just had the very last piece."

He hiked himself up onto his elbows and stared at her. Her lips were tightly compressed. He saw precisely how she had painted him into a corner, and admired the skill of that particular ploy. If he objected, then all the other reasoning was hollow.

"I think that would be a very good idea, Dawn. I know how tough it is going to be, seeing each other every day in the office and wanting each other all the time. It will be a test of character. But I agree one hundred percent. After all, we don't want to cheapen our relationship, do we?"

"No," she said hesitantly. "We certainly don't want that."

Jack Simms and Mike Wasser were inside Feeney's travel trailer by three o'clock, with the white pickup parked outside, and the dog pacing back and forth in its chicken-wire run, growling. An orange power cord ran from the box on the light pole to the outdoor plug on the side of the trailer. The overhead air conditioner whined and sent down a barely perceptible curtain of cool air. They sat under it, Wasser on the bunk and Simms on a blue wooden chair.

"I'd just as soon you don't smoke," Mike said. "It stinks bad enough in here already. Ez isn't real neat."

"Okay," Jack said, grinding the butt out on the vinyl floor. "You're into health, huh? You do weights?"

"Every day."

"Jesus, you look it. I keep thinking I ought to get in better shape." He slapped his belly. "Take off twenty right here."

"Up until about seven years ago I worked on my dad's oyster boat. Then the oysters give out. Coming back now but too late for my old man. He lost the boat, and he lost his feet on account of diabetes. He lives with my aunt over at Galveston. Anyway, we worked the reef shallows with tongs, White House and Pass Christian, like that. You work the tongs all day in twelve feet, you get muscles on your muscles."

"When I used to charter I'd see those boys working the tongs. It didn't look like anything I wanted to try."

"It was the dredges cleaned out the oysters and put us out of business. Now they're seeding the flats from barges and coming back real good, keeping the dredges out of water less than fourteen feet."

"I heard you played football."

"At State. Linebacker. But too slow to get any kind

161

of pro offer. There's too many of those big fast blacks signing up."

"How do you think we ought to do this, with Rowley?"

"I say we let him come right to the door there and knock. It opens in. So I'll open it about six inches and reach out and grab the front of his clothes and yank him inside and pound on him quickly so we don't give him too good a look at us. Suit you?"

"Like Mr. Tuck said, you're in charge. I guess you've done stuff like this for him before."

"If I had, Simms, I wouldn't talk about it."

"Sorry."

"The way I see it, you won't have to do much of anything."

"Suits me. I'm not mad at anybody."

"The way it is, Jack, it's better I do it myself because I know what to do and how much of it to do. I've done it enough times, not for Tuck but for other people. And you take somebody who like you isn't experienced, they can hurt somebody more than they want to."

"Okay."

They waited in an uncomfortable silence. Several times Jack Simms thought he heard a car and he stood and looked out the small window but there was nothing there. Finally when he stood up and looked, he said in a low voice, "BMW four-door coming in, Mike. Parking behind the pickup."

Mike got up, flexed his arms, rolled his shoulders, took a deep breath and huffed it out, and positioned himself near the door. Jack pushed the blue chair out of the way and backed up into the galley alcove to give Mike Wasser room.

When the rap came on the door, Mike pulled it open quickly, reached and snatched the blue sports shirt of the man standing on the step and yanked him in, spinning as he did so to bang the door shut with his shoulder. The man clamped his forearms across the back of Mike's hand and bent forward very quickly, the pain and pressure bringing Mike down to his knees. The man straightened, releasing the pinned right hand, and kicked Mike solidly in the solar plexus. The bigger man collapsed, groaning. One of those, Jack thought, and he stepped forward and hit the man solidly on the side of the jaw with a swinging right hand, knocking him back against the closed door. The man kicked Jack in the kneecap. Mike was sufficiently recovered to reach out and grab the man's ankles and yank his feet out from under him. The man fell heavily and Jack Simms, yelling pain and anger, stepped forward and tried to stomp the man in the face, but the man was trying to elude the kick and it caught him in the throat. The man scuttled backward and sat up, leaning against the door. He put both hands to his throat. He made a single ragged breathy noise. His eyes bulged and his mouth opened wide. His face darkened slowly as his chest heaved in an effort to breathe. The staring eyes looked through them and beyond them. His hands fell away from his throat. He slid slowly over onto his left side and lay still.

"Jesus God, you killed the son of a bitch!" Mike said.

"Shut up, shut up, shut up!"

"That's why I didn't want you messing into it."

"Shut your goddamn mouth! Let me think."

Jack walked back and forth, limping badly, trying to work the pain out of his knee. He eased himself down beside the body and with obvious reluctance, rolled the man over and tugged his wallet out of his left hip pocket.

"This isn't even Rowley," Jack said softly. "This here is Bern Gibbs, Tuck's friend."

"Wow," Mike Wasser said. "Oh Christ. You're in real trouble."

"Look, friend. I didn't kill him. *We* killed him. And it wouldn't have happened if he hadn't come at us with the karate stuff. I stepped in to help because you couldn't handle him."

"Let's settle down. Okay? Just breathe deep. Let's get our heads working. We got a hell of a problem, partner."

Jack opened Feeney's noisy refrigerator and took out two cold cans of beer, tossed one to Mike, pulled the tab on the other and drank deeply. Drank again and finished it and tossed the can in the trash basket. He said, "That BMW is sitting out there like a sore thumb."

"The quicker he's in the trunk, the better I like it."

Jack knelt again, took the cash out of the wallet, shoved the wallet back into the hip pocket. He found the key ring in the right-hand trouser pocket. Mike took the cash out of Jack's hand, counted it, kept half, gave the rest back, and said, "Go open the trunk. Take a good look around. Give me a beep on the horn if it's all clear."

A few minutes later Mike came hurrying toward the car, Bern's body in his arms. He dumped it into the trunk, onto some rope, a couple of Frisbees and a furled umbrella. He folded the legs, pushed them in and slammed the lid down.

"Now where?" Jack asked.

"Shut up a minute." Mike walked down toward the road, stopped and looked across at the sanitary land-fill. Far beyond the fill he could see the backs of some small businesses in a strip shopping area fronting on the highway. Two yellow bulldozers were spreading dirt on the garbage.

He walked back to where Jack stood by the small dark blue sedan. THe old dog started barking. "You got any idea when they stop work over there on the dump?"

"Five o'clock. Then they lock the gates across the access road. It was in the papers. People said it was too early."

Mike looked at his watch. "Forty more minutes. And Feeney don't get off until six. Look around and see if you can find a shovel."

"Can we maybe just pull this thing around behind the trailer?"

"Go ahead."

Simms found a shovel and put it on the floor in back. They waited. Simms said, "I've never been in anything like this before."

"You think it happens every day for me?"

"I didn't mean that."

"Look. We got to stay cool and calm and easy."

"You know what I don't like? I don't like doing it in

165

the daylight. I mean the idea is okay. We dig a hole and put him in where they'll be covering it up tomorrow. But there's kids wandering around here. And people down there by the stores. And cars can come by. It's better we do it at night."

"Let me think on that."

Mike paced for a while. A car went by and they both turned their backs to it. "Okay. Here's what we do. See what you think. We take it out of the trunk and put it over there in the brush out of sight. Then I follow you in the pickup and you drive this car on over to the Bayway Mall and put it in the big—shut up dog!—put it in the lot there and lock it and we drive back to Parklands and give Feeney back his car and tell him the man never showed up. We wouldn't be lying. Rowley never did show. Let's put the shovel next to the body. Okay, tonight we come back here with a bottle and call on Feeney. That old fool will drink until he goes under. Then we tote the body and the shovel over there to the dump and bury it, put the shovel back where you found it, and nobody is ever going to know what the hell happened to Mr. Gibbs."

"Except you and me."

"And we're not talking about it, ever. Drunk or sober, not a word, ever. Right? You talk and we go to prison and I get you killed the first week."

"I'm scared, Mike. I'm really scared. That damned Feeney and his ideas. He got us into this."

"Wipe the fingerprints off the car. Not that anybody will ever check them. But just to be safe."

"I've got the shakes."

"Shut up and open the trunk, Jack."

They lifted the body out and put it on the hard dirt. Simms went out to where he could check the area. When he whistled, Wasser picked the body up and hurried around the end of the trailer and over into the heavy brush in the neighboring lot. Breathing hard, he shoved the body deeper into the bushes. Simms brought the shovel and they put it beside the body. They had to go back to the body and search for the man's keys.

It was a fifteen-minute drive in late-afternoon traffic to the Bayway Mall parking lot. Simms was glad to see the white pickup following him closely. He found a parking lot, parked, and trotted to the pickup and got in quickly.

"You got the keys?" Mike asked.

"Look, that's a forty-thousand-dollar machine. I left the keys in the ignition and the doors unlocked. Somebody takes it, it makes the investigation tougher. And you can bet your ass there is going to be one hell of an investigation of this."

Once they were a mile away from the mall, they both felt better. When they got to Parklands they waved at Feeney as he let them through the gate, parked the white truck and took the keys back to Feeney.

"False alarm, pal," Jack Simms said. "The man never showed up."

Feeney registered disappointment.

"We'll get him next time. We ought to lay some plans," Mike said.

John D. MacDonald

"Plans?"

"You going to be there tonight? Me and Simms, we'll stop by after dark and bring a bottle and sit around and lay it all out, okay?"

"Fine by me," Feeney said, grinning, showing his popcorn teeth.

10

Ezra Feeney, as was to be officially established on the following day, was relieved of gate duty at ten after six on September ninth, and arrived at his travel trailer at about six-thirty.

On his way home he thought about his new friends, Jack Simms and Mike Wasser. It made him feel good to think that they were going to come around this evening and bring a bottle and drink with him. It had been a long time since he'd had friends like them, younger fellows, all muscle and spunk. It bothered him that he had some kind of problem making friends. He knew he was friendly and open and he smiled a lot. He found it easy to talk to strangers, and they seemed to enjoy talking to him. He knew he had a lot of interesting stories to tell. He had been all over the country, working every kind of job you could imagine. He would think he had made a new friend, but after a month or so the new friend would kind of drift away, make excuses. He knew he didn't say any mean things, or do any mean things. He was always willing to loan out anything he owned except his dog. But here these fellows were being real friendly. Maybe, he thought, it was because he'd been born right here in West Bay, and that made some kind of difference. Maybe it was time to put his roots down for good. Stop roaming. Maybe start going to church for the first time in thirty years. When the boys came around this evening he would tell them about his daddy getting squashed when they launched the big boat, right here in West Bay.

He parked under the big tree in his usual spot. It was about an hour to sunset and the shadows were long. Fred was pacing back and forth behind the chicken wire, whining and doing his little welcome dance. When Ezra let him out, Fred scooted for the bushes. Ezra went to unlock his trailer door and found the boys hadn't locked it when they left. He was annoyed. He had told them twice. There was a gang of black teenagers who scavenged the dump and roamed the area and sometimes trashed empty houses.

He had stripped off his sweaty shirt and locked his gun in the bin under the sink when he heard Fred carrying on. He hurried out to see what was going on. There was old Fred over in the lot, aiming his muzzle at the sky and going AAhOOOO, AAhOOOO. It was like some kind of wolf, and he'd never heard Fred do that before. Maybe he had waited too long to go, and he'd busted something.

Ezra trotted over to the dog and pushed through the

brush and stopped abruptly when he saw the shovel and a pair of shiny black shoes and black socks. He knew it was his shovel from the pattern of the worn-off red paint on the handle. The dog kept making the same spooky racket. He pulled a big branch aside and bent over and looked down at a blue-gray face, at eyes bulging, at a death look of strain and agony fixed in place forever, and at the two-way traffic of small red ants going in and out of the corner of the open mouth. His breath huffed out of him. He straightened and the branch snapped back.

Moments later he was running full tilt down Lamarr Street, right down the middle, his leather soles slapping the pavement, a tall scrawny man naked to the waist, all fishbelly white except for the forearms and hands and face and nape of neck. He took long strides as he ran down toward the row of tract houses on Pearson. About every half-dozen strides he would jump a little higher and yell, "Hey!" Fred, the dog, ran beside him, tongue lolling, too quickly winded to bark, but enjoying the change.

Wade Rowley's back had been troubling him lately, giving him sharp twinges in the left leg and making the left foot feel semi-numb as if he were wearing a wet sock on the foot and ankle. Dr. Levering had advised him to swim as often as he could, swim lazy laps and slow turns to keep his back and belly muscles in shape to support the spine. Levering said it was one of the diseases of desk work, of the sedentary civilization.

And so, an hour after dinner, he had donned swim trunks and slid into the pool. As he swam, he went over and over the split with Bern, wondering how much of it was his own fault. Bern wasn't overly tricky for a man of his time and place. Do unto others before they do it unto you. There were a lot of greasy little moves that were just this side of the law. At least he had not let Bern talk him into setting up that real estate syndicate thing as a tax shelter to peddle to their more successful friends and acquaintances. The way Bern wanted to do it would have brought on a lot of audits in the future, and alienated a lot of people, including possibly the S.E.C. Bern wanted to get too big too fast. He wanted to hear people whispering about him when he walked into a room.

Wade decided the split was inevitable. The partners had been alike in their aims for a long time, and then had begun to diverge. No need for any guilt. His own attitudes, compared to Bern's, were as Bern had told him, old-ladyish. Too careful. Too proper.

The divergence had begun, he guessed, four years ago when Bern'd had a buyer for the Maxwell place on the Hungerford Road. All the land had been sold off except for the five acres surrounding the main house. A retired couple from Scranton, Pennsylvania, had made an offer. Bern was writing up the contract. He had told them everything about the house, all the leaks and cracks and the few areas of rot. They loved it.

"Did you tell them about the well?"

"What about the well?"

"The water analysis. The contaminants in the groundwater."

"It's up to them to check the water supply."

"If we had no chemical analysis on file, we would

recommend they have the water analyzed. But when we have the analysis on file . . ."

"Who do you think we're working for?"

"For the seller. And we are not going to willfully conceal any defect we know about in what we sell. We are not in a buyer-beware line of work. We have a public reputation and we have a state license and we are not going to lose either or both. I won't allow it. Go give them a copy of the analysis or I will."

That was where it began, with Bern glaring at him, so angry Wade had wondered if Bern was going to use some of that fancy oriental unarmed combat on him. And that was the year Bern bought his first expensive car, the red German one, the Porsche.

No move could have saved the partnership. It was like a marriage gone bad. Mutual respect had slowly eroded. So don't sweat it. Roll with it. After the Loomis mess is over, make a date for a conference with Rick Riker. It would be a relief to be on his own after these last years of strain. Things were looking up. Beth had agreed with him that the boy was acting a little bit more like himself. He wasn't whole yet, but the direction was up and that was promising enough for now. And Beth seemed less terrified of the future and the possibility of insecurity.

As he made a turn at the deep end, he saw Beth leading two men out onto the screened patio area. The light was behind them so he did not recognize the larger man until he was quite close. Then he saw that it was another high-school classmate, Chet Fairchild, Deputy Chief of the West Bay police.

"Hey, Chet. What's going on?"

"Just a little routine. This here is a new man on the city force, Tommy Landrum, Skid Landrum's middle boy."

Wade, holding to the side, reached up a wet hand and said, "Glad to meet you, Tommy."

The plump young man hesitated, looked at Chet. Chet nodded, so the boy shook the wet hand.

Wade frowned and swam to the shallow end and came up the steps, picked up his big towel and dried his head, face and shoulders as he headed for the poolside table and chairs. "Come have a seat. Can we offer you a brew?"

"Maybe when we get this routine done," Chet said. He sat heavily and looked at Beth and said, "Miz Beth, I'd like for you to stay right here too if you don't mind."

"Sure," she said, and sat down in the fourth chair, looking puzzled.

Chet took out his notebook, opened it to a blank page, tested his ballpoint, and then wrote "Wade Rowley—Sept 9—9:15" at the top of the page. "What I want you should tell me is just where you've been since noon, and who you were with all that time."

"Why?"

"It's better the why comes later. Along with the beer."

"Okay. It hasn't been what you'd call a real exciting day. At noon I was in the office. I had correspondence to catch up, so I was in my office dictating to Ellie Service. We both left at the same time, about twelve-thirty, maybe a little before. She went to her car and I walked four blocks toward the center of town and went to Patsy's for lunch. I had arranged to meet Garry Bowden there. I waited at the bar and he came in at one o'clock, about. He wanted my advice on what's really a banking problem. It's a confidential matter so if he says I can tell you about it, I will. You know Garry. He doesn't like his business affairs talked about all over town. That's why he deals with me on things that aren't really in my field. He had two drinks at the bar and then we got a table in the back and we stayed right there solving all the problems of the world until two-thirty, about. The place was nearly empty when we left. Let me see now. Yes, he drove out of his way and dropped me off at Mississippi Title Insurance. I was dropping in on Dudley Hooker in hopes he'd see me, and if he was out or busy, I figured I could get the information I wanted from one of his girls. But he was in and he said if I'd wait ten minutes he could see me. So I was in his office until quarter to four, I would say, talking about some of the closings that we have coming up, and about a little ongoing dispute he's been having with Rick Riker. That was some dust I wanted to get settled because it was all due to a misunderstanding on Bern's part, and he's too stubborn to go smooth it over. I would guess it is about a mile from there back to my office and I walked it as fast as the heat would allow and got there a little after four o'clock. By then Ellie had a lot of the letters typed and so I read them and signed them. Then I dictated the rest of the letters for her to type up tomorrow morning. And from then until I left at five-fifteen or so, I sat in my office and read over the computer reports for last week, and marked some things I wanted to talk to people about.

One or two phone calls came in for me, so unimportant I can't remember who or what. I got home here at five-thirty and read the part of the paper I hadn't finished this morning, looked at the evening news, had a drink with Beth, and then we had dinner with the kids and I finished *Time* magazine and then I got into the pool there where you came upon me, Chet."

Chet sighed, closed the notebook, put the pen away. "You understand that it's pure routine I got to check this out with Garry and Dudley and Ellie Service, but I know you well enough to know I believe you did exactly what you say you did."

"What the hell is going on, Chet?"

"Let's start with the beer."

"Coming up," Beth said. While she was gone, they talked about what a hot dry year it had been, and how maybe a big whirly would come up out of the Gulf and soak the landscape.

She brought three chilled mugs from the freezer and three bottles of dark Pauli Girl. Chet poured, quaffed, wiped his mouth with the back of his hand and thumped the mug down. All eyes were on him.

"Bern Gibbs has been killed dead," he said.

Beth clapped her hand over her mouth and closed her eyes, shutting out the world of bloody surprise.

Wade said, "I was going to ask if it was in that damn car, but from what you've been asking me, it was some other kind of death."

"Murdered by person or persons unknown."

"Does Nita know?" Beth asked quickly.

"She had to I.D. the body about an hour ago. Her mother and her sister and her girl, they're at her house with her, so I guess she's being cared for. The doctor gave her mother some pills for her. Now I don't want you, Wade, or you, Miz Beth, to get the wrong idea about Nita. But the reason I came here right off was on account of she told me that Bern and you are on the outs, and Bern was so mad at you the other night he told Nita he wanted to kill you. She said she never saw him so mad. And I've heard it around town, can't remember where, that you two weren't getting on real fine. That right?"

"*Damn* her!" Beth said.

"It's okay," Wade said. "She told the truth. He swung on me the other day and I ducked and he hit me right here over the ear. I saw stars. He thought he'd broke his hand."

"You hit back?"

"I was too surprised to get mad, Chet. He was hopping around, hugging his hand, and I wanted to laugh, but if I'd laughed he'd have had to try to kill me. Where did it happen?"

"A weird old boy named Ezra Feency reported it in by phone at eleven minutes before seven tonight. He came off work and let his dog out and his dog found the body in the bushes of the lot just west of his, over on the dirt extension of Eighteenth Avenue off Lamarr. He had to run down to Lamarr to borrow the use of a phone. There'll be an autopsy, but the doc says it looks to him like the cause of death was his getting hit right here in the goozle with a hard object with an edge on it. It mashed the gristle and so on in his throat so as he couldn't breathe and so he strangled to death. Terrible look on his face. Sorry, Miz Beth. Wade, what are you looking funny about?"

"I know Feeney. I was out at his travel trailer back in July. Bern arranged for our firm to process some deeds based on sales on Bernard Island made by Tucker Loomis and company. I wondered if everybody on the list could afford hundred-and-fifty-thousand-dollar lots way out there, and Feeney was the only one I checked on personally. I did a credit check and found three others who couldn't afford that kind of land either. They all worked for Loomis. Feeney is a gate guard out at Parklands. I thought some of those deeds were kinky, and they went through our office, so I was checking."

"You tell Feeney why you were checking?"

"No. I made up some kind of a cover story. He gave me a beer. He certainly didn't seem like any kind of a killer."

"Did Bern carry much cash around with him?"

"Usually two or three hundred."

"He had three ones in a side pocket and some change. He either went out there or he was taken out there. You know any reason why he'd go out to see Feeney?"

"I don't really know. He knew I'd picked up on the phoney purchasers probably by some kind of credit check. Maybe he guessed I'd seen Feeney and he wanted to know what I'd told him. There's another possibility too. I turned the information on the fake land sales over to a friend in the Park Service who turned them over to the U.S. Attorney. The court case is day after tomorrow. Maybe Bern went out there to tell Feeney that if he was subpoenaed, he better keep his mouth shut."

"One funny thing. There was a shovel next to the body. Feeney identified it as his, out of the tool box on the back of his trailer. It was there all ready, as if somebody was going to come after dark and bury the body. There's a good handy place there to bury a body. Right in the dump. Right ahead of where they're tamping it down and spreading the dirt over it. Safer than making a grave in undisturbed land. Feeney said the tool box on the back of his trailer was unlocked and the shovel had been in there. That's not a good neighborhood to leave things unlocked. Of course he's got that big old dog, but the dog is behind wire. Feeney just hasn't any kind of damn idea why there was a body in that lot, and he didn't know who it was."

"Was Bern's car there?"

"We put the tag number and the make and color on the wire. No report on it at the time I left."

"That's an isolated neighborhood on account of the landfill. A forty-thousand-dollar automobile might strike somebody as worth killing for."

"Could be. We got to trace where Bern was all afternoon. We've got a tentative time of death between two-thirty and five-thirty. Know what his schedule was?"

"No. Dawn Marino might know. She was his secretary."

"We've got an address on her but she's not there, at least she wasn't there at nine o'clock. I picked up a rumor that she and Bern had something going. You know about it?"

"I guess everybody at the office had that idea."

"The Marino woman have a husband or a boy-friend?"

"Not that I know of. No husband certainly."

"Mrs. Gibbs know about his his fooling around?"

Beth answered, "She suspected. Just as she suspected the ones before Dawn Marino. But she just wouldn't let herself find out for sure. Because then she would have had to take steps. And she didn't really want to. Not until their daughter Lois was out of the house. I think she was still in love with Bern anyway. No matter what he did."

"She confided in you?"

"Sort of. Not flat out. Just hints and so on," Beth said.

Fairchild turned back toward Wade. "Just what will happen now with your agency? In a financial way."

"Is that part of the investigation, Chet, or are you just curious?"

"I'm looking into motive. I don't think personally you did a thing, Wade. I'm here drinking your beer and talking straight. Business partners have been killed for the way the insurance was written. And killers have been hired."

"The way we set it up, we carry five-year renewable term on each of us. If I remember, it is now at three hundred and twenty-five thousand. Each of us, each of the only two shareholders, agreed in writing that in the event of death, the stock would revert to the surviving partner and the insurance proceeds would go to his heirs for the purchase of that stock. So right now I own the whole thing and Nita gets the three hundred and twenty-five. And as long as we're talking straight here, let me tell you I feel sick at heart at this happening to Bern, and at the same time I feel a sense of relief that we don't have to go around and around for months and months fighting over how to split the damned business up."

"Okay. That's sure straight enough. Who do you know that's going to feel real good about him being dead?"

After about twenty seconds of thoughtful silence, Wade said, "There were those in town who didn't care too much for Bern. And there were some who felt he'd tricked them in one way or another, cut too big a slice of pie. But nobody who'd want to kill him."

"How about somebody wanting to beat up on him?"

"Plenty of those. It's been tried a couple of times, but he took a couple of years of karate lessons at the Y and it didn't work out too great for those who tried it."

"And if somebody tried to stomp him a little after knocking him down, and he was rolling out of the way, it could have got him right here in the Adam's apple."

"I guess it could happen that way."

"So whoever set him up had to know Feeney was working until six and lived close by to the landfill." Fairchild sighed and stood up, folding his notebook. "Thanks for your time and cooperation, folks. Come on along, Tommy. We got more calls to make."

"Yes sir!"

"Night, Miz Beth. Think of anything else, Wade, you call me."

After the Deputy Chief drove out, the phone rang

It was Brud Barnes calling from the city room of the *Courier Journal*. "Hey, Wade? You hear about Bern?"

"Chet Fairchild just paid us a call."

"It was on the ten o'clock news a little while ago. Hell of a thing. No leads yet, they said. I was wondering if—"

"Look, we're pretty shook by this thing, Brud. I can't say anything meaningful abot it. It's a terrible tragedy."

"I was just wondering if it could have anything to do with the Bernard Island deal."

"What? How the hell could it have?"

"How do I know? Feeney works for Loomis."

"And Bern was in Tuck's pocket all the way."

"Can we talk?"

"Later. Maybe tomorrow."

Beth sat on a footstool in the living room, elbows on her knees, her hands combed back into her hair. She looked up at him, her expression rueful. "Why am I feeling guilty?"

"We've both been wishing him bad luck for a couple of years honey. Drop dead. Get out of the way. Stop being so tricky. Stop making trouble. Do your job and shut the hell up."

"Then Nita is feeling guiltier than either of us. I'll have to go see her tomorrow."

The phone rang again. This time it was Helen Yoder. "Wade? Helen. Did you hear about it?"

"Yes. I heard but I don't believe it yet."

"Neither do I. I'll go into the office tomorrow and he'll be there like he always is. Jeanie heard it on the news and phoned all of us. She got hold of everybody

182

except Dawn and you. Your line was busy. She'll probably try you again."

"How about you call her and tell her we've been told, okay?"

"Sure. What do you make of it?"

"So far it doesn't make any sense."

"He called me in and asked me if I'd please stay with him when you two split up. He didn't want an answer right away. Good thing. He wouldn't have liked my answer. Someday I'll tell you why."

He told her he'd see her in the office tomorrow. After he hung up he felt restless. The kids came home; they had heard about Bern. They had a lot of questions he couldn't answer. They were awed that someone they knew had been killed. An adult person. They knew kids who had died—car smashes, motorcycle accidents, drownings, overdoses, suicides—but respectable adults seemed immune to that sort of random violence. He wasn't exactly Uncle Bern, but he was a familiar figure to them. Why would anyone kill a real estate person?

Beth was getting ready for bed. He dressed and went in and told her he was going down to the office.

"Why!"

"I wondered if there might be something on or in Bern's desk or in his office that I could tell Chet about."

"But I don't *want* you going down there at night, not this night. I want you here."

"Honey, it will take just a little while. There's no open season on the owners of Rowley/Gibbs. And I

183

won't be able to sleep unless I take a look. Want to come along?"

She bit her lip, thought about it, shook her head. "But you won't be long?"

"Forty-five minutes. Back before midnight."

The overhead fluorescents were on in the main room of the offices, as they should have been. When he unlocked the front door and went in, the delay began whining at him, ceasing when he punched out the five-digit combination on the little panel off to the side. He walked through to Bern's big office and stopped ten feet from the desk and took a deep breath. The man's presence was tangible, underlined by the pictures of wife and daughter, the framed civic awards, the stationary Exercycle over in the corner, the hole-in-one golf ball on the desk, mounted on a little mahogany pedestal with brass plaque proclaiming the course, the hole, the date.

He went around and sat in Bern's chair, in front of the big mural of the county. He sat quietly for several minutes, and then began looking through the papers, finding nothing of any particular significance. The desk calendar page for the day was nearly blank. There was a single word written in at ten o'clock. "Bank." At twelve-thirty there was a penciled "D.M." The rest of the day was blank. The desk drawers were locked. He did not think they would reveal anything of great interest. He knew he had not expected to find anything. He had wanted to go to the place he had shared with Bern, because that was where he would feel the loss most deeply. That was where Bern's absence would be felt most acutely.

There was no great sense of loss. Just a drifting sadness, a regret that they had ended up so far apart. Had Bern died five years ago the loss would have been painfully sharp, shocking.

He turned the desk lamp off and walked slowly toward the front door. He was aware of a figure outside the door, close to the glass, the silhouette of a woman with the streetlights behind her. He unlocked the front door and Dawn Marino lurched against his chest with such force he was knocked off balance for a moment.

"Oh God, oh God, oh God!" she said in a small hoarse voice.

"There there," he said, aware of the stupidity of the required words, "There there, Dawn." She was shivering. She wore baggy slacks, boots, an earth-colored blouse far too big for her.

"It's my fault," she said in a shaky voice.

He reached around her and relocked the door and then led her to his office. He turned on the lights and backed her up until the edge of the upholstered chair hit the backs of her knees, then lowered her into the chair. She was in the full slant of overhead light then, and her appearance shocked him. She was not the overenameled Miss Tits Marino who had always regarded him with a heavy-lidded insolence, and who had managed to do any chore he gave her slowly and badly. Her eyes were puffed and red, her dark hair tangled, her lips pallid. She looked about fourteen years old.

He put the Kleenex box where she could reach it.

"I've just been driving around," she said. "Since I heard. I tried to see him but they wouldn't let me. They were cutting him open. Oh, Jesus!"

"Why was it your fault?"

Her mouth twisted into an ugliness. "I got too fucking cute, that's why. Nobody was here but Jeanie and me, and this man that wanted you, he wouldn't let Jeanie turn him off, so she put the call through to me and I said I was your secretary. So he gave me the message for you. You were to be at Feeney's at four. Pretty soon Bern came in and we went off together and I told him about the message and how I hadn't left it on your desk. I knew he was really mad at you about Feeney and the other three, the way we had to get their names off the records after you gave copies of the deeds to the Park Service, and so he decided he'd keep your date and see what was going on. We had to go back to the office to get Feeney's address. If I did what I was supposed to do, he wouldn't be dead."

"And I would be?"

She had been looking into an interior distance. She turned and focused on him, licked her lips. "He was going to marry me."

He stopped himself in time. No point in telling her that Bern would never have left Nita. Not for Dawn, nor for any of the undying loves who had preceded her. Bern needed women as a quick polish for his self-esteem. He had to think of himself as desirable to women. A wife didn't count. They had to be in bed, entwined, nose to nose, looking at him with big wet adoring eyes, breathing their moist quick breathing, squirming their loins against him, saying love . . . love.

So if it helped her to keep on thinking he was really going to marry her, let her believe it. Bern had always had a certain elegance in the way he moved, the way he wore his clothes. Women enjoyed looking at him.

"Dawn, have you got anybody you can stay with? Or anybody who can stay with you?"

"I don't know. I can't think of anybody."

"How about Helen?"

"I wouldn't want to ask her."

"Do you know where she lives?"

"Yes. I was there once. It was sort of an office party."

"I'll call her."

"Maybe she's asleep."

He had the number on his Rolodex. She answered on the third ring. Her voice sounded blurred and far away.

"What's your position on taking in the walking wounded, Helen?"

"Wade? Let me try to wake up. I took a Valium. You don't mean you, do you? If you do, any time. Any time at all."

"It's Dawn."

"I don't like the little hairbag, but I'll take her in."

"She's pretty shattered. Bern was going to marry her."

"Ho ho ho and ho."

"That's why this has hit her so hard. She thinks it's her fault. She'll tell you why."

"You mean she is right there with you and I am to go along with this marriage crap?"

"If you don't mind."

"When I try hard, I can believe anything. And I've done it hundreds of times."

"She'll be along soon."

"Put her on."

He gave the phone to Dawn. She said "Yes" several times, nodding each time she said it, and then said "Goodbye" and hung up.

He came around the desk as she stood up. She sobbed once and lunged into his arms again. He held her. There was no tension in it, no passion. It was like holding a tired child. She was spent. He went out with her, set the alarm system, locked up and walked her to her car. The street was empty. He patted her on the shoulder as she got in. "Thanks for . . . for everything," she said.

He watched the red taillights of her small car go two blocks down the empty street and turn left, toward Helen's condo. He walked to his own car, then leaned against the driver's door and looked up at the night sky, at stars hazed by city glow and city smog. A night sky Bern had not seen, to be followed by an infinity of night skies he would never see. He felt an interior twisting, a hollowness of dismay, as he remembered some of the antic times. Bern in a good mood was a very funny man, quick of wit, sour of tongue. In the old days he'd been able to laugh at himself. But not lately.

Headlights startled Wade as the almost silent car pulled up beside him. The officer in the passenger seat said, "Is anything the matter here?"

"No. No thanks. I was just about to go home. I just left that office there. I . . . own the business."

There was a long pause as the man looked him over. "Good night, sir," he said and the patrol car moved away.

Ten years ago, Wade thought, I would have known him and he would have known me. Too many people moving down into the Sun Belt. Too many people moving near warm water. Everything gets diluted. Old friends in the same town and you never see them anymore. The world gets more impersonal. More people stay close to home.

It was a change in the way people live these days, he thought. They are out there in their little frame houses in the developments, racially segregated by choice, not by edict. They live in their houses and in their cars. They rent tapes of movies, and the streets are empty after dark.

He drove home slowly. Beth was feigning sleep. He knew she was annoyed he had taken so much longer than he had promised.

At a few minutes past three on Wednesday morning, thirty miles past Montgomery, Alabama, on Interstate 85, a state police patrol car tried to intercept a dark blue BMW traveling at an estimated hundred miles an hour. In pursuit, with the speedometer steady at a hundred and fifteen and the BMW slowly increasing the distance between the two cars, the pursuing patrol car radioed for help, giving the position as just past Exit 38, suggesting a roadblock, describing the car and saying they had not gotten close enough to read the tag.

Two cars went into position southwest of the Opelika Exit 60, all lights spinning and flashing, blocking the northeast lanes down to a single lane, all personnel out of the vehicles, shotguns ready to shred the tires if the speeding car tried to run the block. They let three interstate trucks through, and then in the silence saw the oncoming lights and heard the faraway keening of the pursuing siren.

The oncoming car slowed somewhat, and then, about two hundred yards short of the roadblock, it went to the left, off the highway and down into a drainage swale, came up the far side and became air-borne. As the awed officers watched, it made a slow roll, left to right, in the air. It was obvious to them that the driver had hoped to cut across the median to the southwest-bound lanes, clear the block and then come back to the northeast lanes. The car went to a height they had never seen a car reach before. It gave the strange impression of something floating.

"Son of a *bitch*!" said Officer Caffrey, a twenty-year veteran, using profanity for the first time since being born again ten years earlier.

The car landed upside down on the far lane, bounced up again looking oddly flattened, whirled and bounded end for end off a slope and down, down to the Exit 60 underpass, crossed Route 280 and came to rest in a tiny patch of slash pine in front of an animal hospital. The law gathered around, put the spotlights on it, sprayed foam where needed, summoned the jaws of life, in this case misnamed, and cut and pried the two bodies out of something that no longer even looked like an automobile. They were two young males, estimated age seventeen to nineteen. One of them had some limited identification on him—Armando Hernandez of Metairie, Louisiana. They found it in his left hip pocket which seemed to be all too close to his right armpit. The BMW had been licensed in Mississippi, and the numbers were on the computer file as wanted in connection with a murder in West Bay.

Before going off duty at six in the morning, Officer Caffrey held forth to his captive audience of fellow officers in the squad room of the state police barracks.

"What it comes down to," he said, "is all this jumping automobiles around on the TV. These pointy-headed kids, they don't know about it's always special cars, special conditions. Now you take the average vee-hikel, you jump that mother ten feet from here to there, and what you got, you got like a four-hundred-dollar repair bill and you prolly got a whiplash to go with it."

11

A bad dream jolted Wade Rowley awake at five, after a very few hours of sleep. The dream faded before he could recapture any part of it. It left him sweaty and shaky. He got up quietly, showered and dressed and went in and kissed Beth on the temple. She rolled over and opened her eyes.

"Wha' you doing up?"

"Couldn't sleep. I'll go in and get caught up on a couple of things. You go back to sleep."

"I don't think I can now."

When he looked in on her before leaving she was buzzing softly, breathing deeply and slowly.

The sun wasn't up by the time he got to Ezra Feeney's trailer. In the gray morning light Feeney was backing his white pickup toward the travel trailer. Fred was in the bed of the pickup, as was the thick roll of chicken wire and the posts from his daytime jail.

Feeney gave him a quick glance and got out of the pickup and went back and, with a great straining effort, lifted the trailer cup onto the ball of the hitch on the back of the pickup.

"What are you doing?"

"What the hell does it look like to you?"

"I'd say you were leaving."

"Bet your ass," Feeney said. He made the hitch fast, then made the electrical connections for the taillights and brake lights on the trailer. "Get in and step on the brake while I check."

Fred rumbled at him as Wade got in. When he stepped on the brake Feeney yelled, "Okay."

When Wade got out he said, "What went on here yesterday?"

"What went on here? I come back from work and found me a dead man over in the lot and I reported it in. That's what went on."

"Isn't there more than that?"

"If there was, I wouldn't talk to you about it. The last time I talked to you, you told me that damn lie about ten thousand dollars. You think I wouldn't remember that? You made a fool of me. If I was ten years younger, I'd be hammering on you right now."

"If anybody made a fool of you, Ezra, it was Tuck Loomis."

"I don't see that."

"He had you sign papers that didn't mean anything. The papers were lies that could get you into trouble with the law."

"I worked for him and did like he said."

"The police know you're leaving?"

"They didn't ask and I didn't tell them."

"Why *are* you leaving?"

Feeney pulled a flat can out of his pocket, took a thick pinch of shredded tobacco and tucked it deftly behind his lower lip. The sun's first rays shone on the truck and the trailer and the sitting dog. It shone on the beard stubble on the side of Feeney's face.

"I wasn't born yesterday. I've got a lot of miles on me, mister. I can tell when I got fair-weather friends, smiling around, bringing booze, making up to me, setting me up for trouble. Yes sir. I figure this place was bad luck for my daddy and I am leaving before it turns into the same kind of bad luck for me."

"You expect to get killed here?"

"I wouldn't put it past."

"Past who?"

"I'm not going any further than that, mister."

"Let me ask you one thing."

"Why should I?"

"I don't know. I'll ask it and you can decide if you want to answer. Should I be worried about myself? Was I in any danger yesterday? Can I be in any danger in the future?"

"Maybe there was a little something going on. Maybe on account of your tried to mess into Mr. Tuck's business affairs somebody could have wanted to bump you around a little. Sort of quiet you down. I mean it could have been like that."

"And they bumped Mr. Gibbs around instead?"

"I didn't say anything like that. Look, I meant to be on the road by sunrise, mister. I want six hundred miles of road between here and wherever by night time. I don't want to be around here in case somebody thinks I figured out more than I should."

He got in and slammed the door, started the motor. He whistled and Fred jumped down and trotted around to the passenger door. Feeney reached and opened it for him and closed it after he was in. The dog sat on the seat, his head on the same level as Feeney's. They both looked at Wade through the driver's window, and he thought there was much the same expression in each pair of eyes—a weary, road-worn hostility, an habitual suspicion.

The trailer rocked and lumbered down to the drive. Feeney got out, uprooted his mailbox and put it in the trailer bed next to the chicken wire. He got back in and drove away, turning up Lamarr toward the state highway and the Interstate.

At nine-thirty Chet Fairchild and Wade Rowley and Detective Lieutenant Al Himmer were in Bern Gibbs' office, going through the drawers and the files in a search that seemed to Wade to be aimless, as were the questions they asked him.

"And she won't be in at all?" Chet asked.

"I don't know. She's at Helen Yoder's apartment. When Helen left she was sleeping. The girl is worn out. This was a big shock to her."

"You know if he tried to break off with her?"

"He promised the girl he would marry her."

Chet sighed. "Well, that's Bern for sure. I guess he always promises that. Eternal love and devotion. For my money, it's one hell of a cheap way to get into a woman's pants."

"I didn't know his hobby attracted that much attention."

"Well, it sort of came out a few years back when the Waters woman cut her wrists. She made a statement. No action to be taken on anything like that. Maybe some kind of civil suit, but that's out of my territory. She moved away somewheres."

A phone call came in for Deputy Chief Fairchild. He sat at Bern's desk to take it. He listened for a time and then said, "What's the other thing?" He listened again and finally said, "You should have told me the last one first, and then you could have skipped the other."

He hung up and shook his head, smiling but exasperated. "Some people got the horse sense of a horsefly. First a big thing about Smitty going out to ask that Feeney some more questions and finds out Feeney has packed up and left, rural mailbox and all. And *then* he tells me they got a report in from the Alabama state police that Bern's BMW turned up over past Montgomery in the small hours. Pair of young latinos in it from the New Orleans area. Got chased for speeding, tried to run a roadblock, flipped the car, totaled it, killed them both. So there's our answer, men. We can stop this rooting around in these here papers."

After Himmer had left, Fairchild and Wade had some coffee in Wade's office. With the door shut, Wade said, "This wraps it up?"

"It does for sure. Saves the taxpayers a lot of money too."

"What if it was somebody else killed him, Chet?"

"That what you really think?"

"I might think that."

Chet stirred more cream into his coffee, took a careful sip and then a large swallow. He looked down at the coffee rather than at Wade. "Let's think on that. You and I, we get the idea that maybe Joe Jones killed Bern. We dig into it. That is, if we can spare the time to do the digging. Lot of police work around these days. Incidentally, we just got turned down on the additional bodies and equipment we need—three days in a row it is. Limits on overtime, too. Okay, we can make a pretty good case against this Joe Jones. Of course he'll know all about the two men dead in Bern's fancy automobile. Suppose we make a case so strong the grand jury will indict and the prosecution will go ahead with it. This Joe Jones hires himself a lawyer. Now when it goes to the jury they are going to be told all about reasonable doubt. If they think it is a reasonable possibility those two fellows killed Bern and took his forty-thousand-dollar car, then they are going to have to let Joe Jones go." He raised his head and looked at Wade, his eyes wise and tired and full of a subdued irony. "All along the line a lot of men are going to think about Joe Jones and what kind of a case we've got against him and what the chances are, and any one of those men can up and say the hell with it, we can't make it stick. So when we get a chance to wrap it up, old friend, we wrap it up tight. Follow?"

"Yes."

"Some wouldn't. They get hung up on truth and beauty and justice and a lot of clever patient tireless police work. Police work is mostly going around cleaning up as many messes as you can. And if you ever get ahead of the day-to-day messes, there's always some open cases you can go back and take another look at. Most of those cases still open would look a lot better than this Joe Jones case. And either way, the widow gets the insurance."

"So you don't think they did it?"

"You're getting to sound like our old classmate, Brud Barnes. Got to go. Thanks for the coffee."

The condemnation proceedings took place in the District Court as scheduled at ten o'clock on Thursday morning, September eleventh. The government's case was presented by two young attorneys from the U.S. Attorney's Office for the district, Frederick Sanders and Oliver Dawkins.

They had been assigned to the condemnation proceedings three weeks prior to the date set for the case.

The appraiser called by the government to testify stated that the highest and best use for the land on Bernard Island was as government park and recreation land, and he gave his appraisal figure as seven hundred and twenty thousand dollars.

The case for the Bernard Island Corporation was presented by attorneys Hubbard Yoder and Robert Thomas Schlesinger, with the assistance of three paralegals, three appraisers, a tabletop model of Bernard Island as it would have looked when developed, a series of slides showing the development of comparable Gulf-front land in the area, along with the assessed value thereof, a history of the sales of land in the vicinity of the Mississippi Gulf Coast along with arm's-length appraisals thereof, a file of the land sales on

Bernard Island with the prices the buyers were willing to pay for the lots. They also qualified certain experts and put them on the stand—an expert in beach erosion and how to limit its damage, a hydrologist, an ecologist and an expert in oceanfront construction.

The Court heard the government's arguments first, and then recessed for lunch, and came back and told the Bernard Island Corporation to present its case concerning the proper value which should be put on the property.

In his opening statement Bobby Tom Schlesinger called the Court's attention to the fact that the United States government had been making ineffective gestures toward taking over all the barrier islands for at least fifteen years, and this uncertainty had played a part in keeping the value of all that land depressed. He also stated that inasmuch as the potential developer had not foreseen any special problem in getting the rights and permissions granted to develop and build on Bernard Island, then the highest and best use was surely oceanfront residential and resort usage rather than national park usage. He said it was their intention to show the Court that by being deprived of their ownership of this land, the stockholders of the corporation stood to lose a minimum of ten million dollars, so that should be the price the government should pay.

The Bernard Island Corporation presentation was continued on the following day, and was completed by four o'clock on the afternoon on Friday, September twelfth. Tucker Loomis, president and principal stockholder in the Bernard Island Corporation, was in attendance both days, having arrived by private jet owned by Regal Construction. He was interviewed by television, newspaper and radio representatives several times during the recesses and at the end of each court day. He said he was confident of fair treatment by Judge Swane, a man he had never met but who certainly had a good reputation in the area. He said he had made himself available for examination by the government attorneys but that they had apparently decided nothing would be gained by questioning him on the stand.

Rather than adjourning the Court at four o'clock, Judge Swane declared a half-hour recess and went to his chambers with a stack of the documents presented by the Bernard Island Corporation. The attorneys and personnel of the Bernard Island Corporation used this interlude to pack up their numerous bulky exhibits, the screen and slide projector, and the cartons of additional documents, and carry them out to the two vans parked near the court house.

During the half-hour recess Judge Swane had written a short statement which he read into the record when Court was readjourned.

"This Court has listened with care to the arguments, statements and testimony of expert witnesses presented by both sides. Certain adjustments have been made in the amount requested by the corporation, reducing the claim finally by fifteen percent on the grounds that it is not probable that the land in question would ever be totally developed, and variations in the going price of land would tend to raise a question concerning the optimum value of land sales reported by the corporation and properly recorded. The most significant factor affecting the Court's decision in this matter is that at no time did the government attorneys raise any objection to the comparable sales data for other areas as presented by the corporation attorneys. It is hereby ordered that the sum of eight million five hundred thousand dollars shall be paid as a proper recompense for the condemnation of the lands in question. This sum is due and payable as of today, and interest on that sum shall begin to accrue as of today."

On Monday afternoon, the fifteenth of September, at quarter past four, J. Harrison Derks met by prearrangement with Sam Loudner at the University Club on the top floor of the West Bay Citizens Bank, N.A., the bank of which Derks was the president. They met in a quiet corner of the lounge, far from the bar.

"He came at me this morning like you said he would, Sam. Came in with Boob Davis, both of them grinning like egg-sucking foxes. Boob said it was the most interesting court case he ever saw."

"How much did he want?"

"Wanted to set up a line of credit for half. Four million two fifty. It's over our limit on him. We'd have to lay it off upstream. Do you think he's going to get that much money?"

"The government will take it to the Fifth U.S. Circuit Court of Appeals. I talked to my boys about it, told them how they done good. Yoder and Schlesinger. From how they tell it, the U.S. Attorney's Office rolled over and played dead. Very strange. That's transient land out there, for God's sake. Those islands are

201

all moving west and north, a little bit every year. Hurricanes put storm surges right over them. Nobody in this county or state would dare give permission to build out there."

"What will happen?"

"Pink, I think the Appeals Court will uphold Swane. With what was put before him, he couldn't come to any other decision. But it can go on a long time before Tuck ever gets the money in hand. The interest on that kind of loan could come to forty-five thousand a month, pretty heavy for Tuck. He likes to live high."

"I don't think I could get it past my board."

"Don't bullshit a bullshitter, Pink. You've got a tame board there and you run a good bank and they'll go along with what you say."

"Well, it's not like we were independent. The name sounds it, sure. But we're on little hunk of the great Sunshine Federated. The only way we could swing it would be if Tuck would put ou six and a half million in good solid collateral, but old Tuck is never going to let any kind of collateral sit idle when he can borrow against it and buy something more that he can use as collateral. He's the original pyramid builder. What I want to know is what you think of the whole thing."

"I can only go on my gut feeling. Tuck is real cute. There is such a thing as being too cute. And there is such a thing as winning too big. I mean a lot of things can bounce back at you sooner or later. Me, I'd stay back."

Derks sighed. "Easiest way is to set up the cover story with Sunshine, then tell Tuck I can't get it approved until the decision comes down on the appeal. That's what I'd have to say to a stranger walking in. But Tuck has been good business for the bank."

"Good business for quite a few people around here."

"But I kind of get that same gut feeling you've got, Sam. Like his walls could come tumbling down. I hate to turn my back on him."

"In more ways than one, maybe. Newspaper has been chewing on him pretty good. You know, when you get enough people pissed at you, somebody is going to find a way to give you a bruise."

"Well, thanks. You've told me what I wanted to hear. I didn't see you at Bern Gibbs' funeral."

"We were all set to go, but at the last minute Ruth got a call from the nursing home that her mother was in a bad way. So we went over there and stayed until ten. The old lady came out of it again, woke up and got cranky and told me I needed a haircut. How was the service?"

"The church was packed. Never saw so many flowers. Imagine getting yourself killed for a damn automobile. I was thinking sitting there in church, if you want a big funeral, die young. Last year when we went to Sid Baker's memorial service, how many were there? Eighteen or twenty? And he was a very big man in this state long ago. He lived to be ninety-three. Goes to show you."

"We don't do criminal law at the shop. I used to get into a little of it years ago. The way they reconstruct it, Bern stopped at the Bayway Mall for something or other. A couple of people reported seeing his car there in the late afternoon. The kids were prowling the mall and moved in on him when he got back into his car. Maybe they held a knife on him. They had him drive out into that fairly empty area near the landfill. They were going to leave him there. He made the mistake of trying to take on the two of them. He got a cracked jawbone and he got kicked in the throat. So they dragged him over into the bushes and they looked around that trailer and found a shovel and they were getting set to bury him when something startled them and they drove off. Is that the way you read it?"

"Pretty much. Yes."

"Why did they take money and not take credit cards? Why did they stick his wallet back in his pocket? Why didn't they drop him off one of our hundreds of bridges? Why did they leave his solid gold wristwatch on? You do criminal law, you get in the habit of looking for holes."

"There's nobody left to answer the questions."

"Bern was working close with Tuck. Now Wade's got the business and I don't think he and Tuck get along too well. So Tuck will probably do his real estate work in house, and go back to Tom French for some of it. Tom is a little too slippery for my taste."

"We don't use him on any bank business anymore. We had some problems."

"In connection with anything Tuck was involved in?"

"Well . . . yes."

"I wondered why Tuck picked up with Rowley/Gibbs. Glad to know the answer."

"And you don't know where it came from."

"Where what came from?"

On Tuesday evening, a week after Bern's death, in the hot stillness of the night, after he had finished his half-hour swim, Wade toweled off and spread his big towel on the twin chaise and settled onto it, sighing. Soon Beth came out and sat beside him.

"Are you kind of down?" she asked.

"I guess so. I spent the whole afternoon with Rick getting the legal stuff straightened away. He kept telling me that having the partnership set up as a Chapter S corporation makes things a lot easier. I couldn't see anything very easy about it. Things are going to be in a mess for quite a while, I guess. Bern didn't keep good records of his prospects and where he was in negotiations. And one account is short about thirty-eight hundred dollars. It loks as if Bern borrowed it and didn't have a chance to pay it back in. Rick says we can pick it up out of the insurance money, but I'd rather just forget it than take it out of Nita. Once she settles Bern's other debts, the income from what's left might be enough for her to keep the house and get Lois through college. Too bad he didn't have any personal insurance."

"Thoughtless and . . . wicked."

"He knew he was going to live forever."

She turned the floor lamp on and looked at a magazine for a little while. He stared out at the night. Finally she put the magazine aside and said, "There's something else wrong, isn't there?"

"What makes you think that?"

"Eighteen years of marriage. Eighteen years of observation."

"It upset me, this whole thing. We worked together for a long time. I had to go through his personal stuff yesterday and throw out some things that I didn't want to send home to Nita. And tear up some letters from women."

"And that's all that's wrong?"

He knew it had to be all. If she were to find out that Bern had been killed by a person or persons who thought he was Wade Rowley, all her insecurity would come floodin back, more than ever.

"Hey, that's all! Isn't it enough. How is Nita handling it? How was she this afternoon?"

"Kind of wan and hollow. But she's got plenty of support around. Her mother and two sisters and a cousin. House full of women. One of the sisters I didn't take to. Molly. She went around looking at the bottoms of plates and vases, like she was shopping. But the other three are fine."

"How about the girl?"

"It's hard to tell. Lois has always been a strange person. When she was little she was daddy's darling. And then about three years ago when she was fourteen she and Bern began to battle. Only child. Love-hate relationship, I guess. I saw her for just a few minutes. She came in from school and changed and went out again, saying she'd be home late. She didn't ask if she could, or tell where she'd be. I wouldn't take that from a kid. Ever."

"Bern was saying lately she's out of control. He said

it in a funny way. Almost as if he was proud of her, as if he encouraged it."

"Tod seems a lot better, don't you think?"

"I haven't seen much of him. Glad to hear it."

"He was good with Lois at the funeral, sitting with her."

"How did he get home?"

"They walked."

"Hell of a long walk."

"Did you set a time for him to get back tonight?"

"No. It's dead calm. He's good with boats. Responsible. And trolling by moonlight is the kind of fishing he likes best. If he goes into a good run he might be pretty late. I think that right now trying to restrict him isn't too great an idea. He wants to be treated like a grown-up because he thinks he's got grown-up problems. And maybe he has. But he's working things out."

"Are you going to get rid of Dawn Marino?"

"I don't know. She came in today and she was a lot of help with Bern's filing system. I think I'll assign her to Bruce Halliday. He's beginning to bring in a hell of a lot of business. As much as Helen and Tom."

"That woman will be trouble wherever she works."

"Right now we need her. She knows the routines. I may let her go after all the hassle is over, but not until I have a replacement lined up."

"What about your own income?"

"I don't have to worry. I have a working wife."

"Seriously. I was wondering."

"I've felt for a long time we were taking too much out of the business. But I had to take what Bern took.

207

We need a lot of things down there. We need another terminal and I want to tie in to a couple of real estate networks. I want to turn Bern's office into two offices. There aren't enough places to have a private conversation. People don't want to sit out in the bull pen and talk dollars. And I want to give some thought to setting up a branch, maybe in Ocean Springs, maybe in Gulfport. So, for maybe a year, Bern's take will be plowed back in, and I'll stay the same."

"Are you going to change the name?"

"Not right away."

 **12**

They had made a nest in the bow of the Whaler, forward of the control pedestal, using a blanket, a tarp, life belts and seat cushions. Tod had anchored in the shallows a hundred yards northwest of the big lagoon on Horn Island, anchored where a sand bar shelved upward and created an area free of any boat traffic so that he would not have to use the anchor light, yet far enough out from the island so that the gentle breeze from the northwest kept the mosquitoes and gnats at bay.

The sunset had ended two hours before, with the last rosy line across the western horizon. It was a night of great clarity and space. The moonlight rested upon them and upon the water. They had watched the blaze of stars, had seen them muted by the increasing moonlight, had seen the quick scoot of three meteors across the night sky. They had talked and talked and talked.

She had wept, many times. They had made pledges to each other, and promises about what life would be like for them, what they would keep and what they would discard. He had showed her the incredible color and richness of the acres of yellow blossoms at four o'clock that afternoon, and they had been together ever since, talking and loving, wanting and giving, knowing that at last in this time and place the two of them had created a single entity that was wiser and warmer and more calm than either of them had ever been when they were alone in what now seemed like some kind of prior existence, barren and pointless.

When he rolled up onto his right elbow and looked down into her large dark eyes in her small face, the nape of her neck fitted his forearm with a preordained perfection. He bent slowly and kissed her lips. Her small breasts were ivory in the moonlight, the nipples shadowed by their own darkness. He bent again and kissed her right breast, touching the nipple with his tongue, feeling it respond. He had lost his awkwardness with her, his fears and his hesitations. He felt as if he could do nothing clumsy with her, nothing wrong.

A little while later he moved over her, holding his weight on his knees, and once again marveled at the mysterious abundance of her. She was such a small girl, quick and light and narrow of waist and hip. But in love she opened to him a great white warmth of thighs and belly, and took him into heated depths, enfolding, encasing, containing, giving a little grunt and sigh of pleasure at the joining, holding him still for a little while to savor that feeling of being one before the slow and gentle and steady movements began, working inevitably to the same climax as before, to the same crescendo of joy.

"I love you, Tod," she said.

"I love you too, Lois."

"No, don't go away from me yet."

"I'll stay right here. Forever."

"Why do you give me the feeling my father has forgiven me?"

"Maybe he has."

"I couldn't feel like this if he hadn't. I know I couldn't."

On that same night Mike Wasser came in through Ship Island Pass, out of the long roll of the Gulf through the tidal current in the Pass and into the relative calm of the Sound. He pushed the throttles forward and brought the *Thelma III* up to cruising speed. Once he got his bearon the northern horizon, he adjusted course to head for West Bay. He set the automatic pilot and then, with a flashlight, carefully checked the cabin and the cockpit deck. In the scuppers he found a leather eyeglass case with a pair of sunglasses in it that had golden brown lenses. He flipped them over the side.

He went back and sat at the wheel, watching it make its small turns to left and right as the compass corrected it. It felt good to him, being out on the water at night. It made more sense than other kinds of life. He wondered if he could go back to oystering. A hired hand. It was a different life these days. A hard life at the best of times. A half hour later he pulled the motors back down, took it off pilot and went into the

bay, followed the markers to the mouth of the Alden
and went up the river to Parklands. It was past one
o'clock and the area was quiet. After he made the boat
fast, he walked over to the dockmaster's office and
once again checked the room behind it where Jack
Simms had lived. Every personal thing and everything
of any value had been packed and removed.

He went out and around to the side and got into
Jack's Torino, and drove down to the gate. He slowed
and gave the night man a look at the windshield me-
dallion. New man on the gate.

Wasser headed north to I-10, turned west and drove
to New Orleans. He turned off at the airport inter-
change, found the long-term parking area, took his
ticket out of the dispenser, drove in and parked. He
wiped the steering wheel, shift lever, headlight control,
rear-vision mirror and door handle. He locked the car
and on the way to the terminal he dropped the torn-up
ticket and the keys into a trash container.

He took a four-fifteen a.m. Greyhound back to
West Bay. At seven-thirty on Wednesday morning he
was back in his small ground-floor garden apartment
near the club, in the only condo structure Mr. Loomis
had permitted to be built at Parklands. He took a long
scalding shower and then sat with a half tumbler of
vodka and ice in front of his small television set until it
was nine o'clock.

Then he phoned the Loomis house. A woman answered and called Mr. Loomis to the phone.

"Good morning, Mr. Loomis. This is Mike."

"Good morning, Mike. What can I do for you?"

"I wondered if maybe I could see you this evening after you get back from town."

"No problem. Is everything all right?"

"Everything is fine. Just fine, sir."

"Glad to hear it. I'll be back early today. Maybe about four o'clock. Come on up to the house about four-thirty."

On Wednesday after lunch at the University Club with a potential client, Wade Rowley started back to the office in his car and then changed direction and went on out to Riverway Homes, halfway to Parklands. Jerry McIntosh owned twenty acres, with a river frontage of a thousand feet. Helen Yoder and Bruce Halliday had worked closely with him, planning his small development. He had permissions for thirty homes on the acreage, and the model house had been finished a month ago. Helen and Bruce had been in on the basic design, the floor plans, the positioning on the lots. Rowley/Gibbs would handle the promotion and sales of the houses at Riverway.

Helen Yoder had fought Jerry McIntosh nose to nose over the selection of the interior decorator and the cost of the decoration of the model home. Helen had won, and she had asked Wade to take a look at the house when he had a chance. Today was one of the days she would be on duty there.

Her old blue and white van was parked on raw earth out beside the carport. No other cars were there. Three other houses were being built. As he got out of his car in the driveway he could hear the whine of electric saws, the sound of nail guns.

213

The front door was open. He knocked and went in. Helen sprang up from a recliner chair in the living room. She wore a yellow jumpsuit and a green scarf knotted at her throat. "Shucks!" she said and snapped her fingers. "Thought I had some more pigeons. Today I've nailed one for-sure and another probable. Jerry's going to have to start some more of these. Want the tour?"

"Sure. It looks nice."

"It *is* nice. A reliable builder and a great floor plan, and the price is right."

He followed her through the three-bedroom, two-and-a-half-bath house, one bath looking as if it had been lifted from the set of *Dynasty*. Some walk-in closets, a two-car carport with automatic doors, a broad screened terrace big enough for a pool, but without one as yet. An electronic kitchen, carpeting throughout, shade trees in the backyard. The flavor of the house was one of serenity, restfulness. The colors were grays and blues and earth tones. There were a few spots of vivid contrast, a white vase of red flowers, a vibrant print on the wall, a dozen pillows in primary colors on a couch. Central air conditioning with a heat-pump assist, upcoming tie-in to the West Bay sewer extension program, a central lake and recreation area available for the use of all the residents.

"And all this is yours, yours, yours for only one hundred and fifty-five five," she said, "convenient terms. Like it?"

"Insulation?"

"State of the art throughout. You are a canny buyer, sir."

"I know some people in the business."

"Come back to the kitchen with me, canny buyer."

She opened the refrigerator and took out an opened bottle of Robert Mondavi Fumé Blanc, a third of it gone. She filled two wine glasses with care, recorked the bottle and put it back. "Here you go, Wade. This is what happens when you say for sure you want one of these here houses."

They sipped, smiling at each other. He was more than ever aware of the vitality of the woman, the restless energy in the way she moved and talked, the way she tossed back that coarse mane of dark blonde hair, the way she tilted her head when she talked to him. She looked trim and abundant, narrow waist, long slender throat, swell of hips and breasts and lips.

"How is it going to work out at the office?" she asked.

"So far I would guess it will be okay."

"Better than that. Better than okay. The tension is gone. Don't you feel it?"

"I've been too busy to feel much of anything."

"Let me tell you that the flavor is good. People are kind of smiling to themselves, you know? We're all going to be a hell of a team. You wait and see."

"I hope so."

"It was a dumb dreary way for Bern to get himself killed. So pointless."

"Maybe there was some kind of a point to it." He didn't know he was going to say it until he said it.

She tilted her head and said, "What do you mean?"

"Forget it."

"No. Come on. I am part of the ball club, friend. I

travel with the team. What do you mean there was a point to it? I've been thinking about it too, you know. You wished Miss Tits Marino on me last Tuesday night, remember. And she had a weird story about Bern keeping an appointment for you out at Feeney's trailer."

He leaned against a countertop. There had been no one to tell, no one to kick it around with, no one who would understand. It had been boiling inside him, seeking outlet. And so as she listened with great intensity, he told her. Matching up Dawn's story and Ezra Feeney's story. And how he had reported the false deeds, and Bern's account of how furious Tucker Loomis had been.

She was standing closer, frowning at him. "So it was Tuck's idea?"

"I'm not saying that. I know you're a friend of his. I don't think he'd be that crude. Besides, it would be an unacceptable risk, wouldn't it? He had everying going his way. I think it was some of his people. He bitched about me so much that some of his people thought they ought to work me over as a favor to him."

"Listen, I know the man. I know him well. He doesn't encourage *anybody* to go ahead and act on their own. He likes his thumb in every pie. He likes to run things, right down to the last inch."

"He wouldn't have expected me to die, you know. Just a physical beating. Enough to make me mind my own business and stop minding his."

"If it had happened that way, would it have worked?"

"On me? No. At least I don't think so. I think I would have gotten a lot more involved. But maybe that's just my picture of myself. Wade Rowley, fearless hero. I've been beat up. But it was so long ago it's hard to remember how I felt, I mean except for feeling sore and sick."

"You haven't told anybody else this whole thing?"

"No."

"Not even Beth?"

"Especially not Beth. She wouldn't handle it very well, thinking people were out to maim her husband."

"Do you think they'll come after you again?"

"I wouldn't think so, but who knows."

She reached over and put her empty wine glass on the counter he was leaning against. She moved closer, looked up into his eyes. She was frowning with great concern. "How awful for you," she said in a husky whisper. "How really awful for you!" She pressed her mouth against his, her arms sliding around him. He put one hand on her waist. It was like touching the housing of some curious engine, a dynamo giving off a throbbing vibration. He felt the long warm weight of her body against him. He held his wine glass in his free hand, with the almost superstitious feeling that all would be well if he did not put it down and put both hands on the woman. The kiss was hungry, and he began to want her very badly indeed, with little pictures of her running through the back of his mind, pictures of her walking away from him, walking past his open office door, getting into her van, laughing, making her strong gestures, tilting her head to toss her hair back.

Suddenly he remembered that first driving lesson when he was fourteen, when his father took him out to a deserted back road and had him get behind the wheel of the Studebaker. The engine was running and he could feel the powerful vibration. He knew how to put it into gear and release the clutch pedal. He was filled with a kind of sick excitement, afraid to drive it and afraid not to.

"Hello!" someone called. "Hello! Anybody home?"

She moved back from him, face flushed, eyes wide, lipstick smeared. "Coming!" she called. "Coming!"

He waited while she showed two women through the house. It took about fifteen minutes. While he waited he thought of a dozen ways to tell her he did not want to get involved.

They sat in the flawless living room. "Saved by the bell," she said, with rueful smile.

"Saved by the hello."

"One of them is coming back to show it to her husband. I say it is about a six on a one to ten scale. Wade, damn it, I'm sorry. I fastened onto you like a leech. What you told me upset me. And I reacted."

"It wouldn't be a great idea. You and me."

"You don't have to tell me that."

"But I can't help thinking of ways we could try to work it out somehow. And that's dumb."

"That's dumb, yes. But flattering. So thank you for that."

"I better go, Helen. Good luck with the project here."

She walked him to the door. They smiled at each other, each knowing all the unsaid things, each aware of the wanting. They shook hands ceremoniously. "There's something I'll probably do about Tuck."

"What do you mean?" he asked.

"Something I should do. I don't want to talk about it. If I do it, you'll hear about it."

13

On Wednesday in the late afternoon, Tucker Loomis sat on a faded blue wooden box three feet square and fifteen feet long. It had been built for little children to crawl through. He had hired carpenters to build the box and put up some other playground toys he had found in a book about suitable outdoor toys for the young. The private playground was in a flat area where his property sloped down to the bank of the Alden River. A hurricane fence had been erected to keep the toddler grandchildren from falling into the river currents. There were swings and a slide and a little whirlygig.

Mike Wasser sat on the bottom of the slide, his shoes in the sand where children had landed. They had talked for a long time. Tucker felt lethargic and depressed, and Wasser seemed sour and defensive.

"The way I see it," Mike said, "there was no choice

at all. I mean every day he was getting jumpier. He was going to crack. He just couldn't handle it. He was going to have to talk about it. We did the only thing we could do. I keep telling myself that."

"Can we go over some of it again?" Tuck asked.

"I don't want to talk about it anymore."

"I want to make sure there's no loose ends."

"There's no loose ends. He's chain-wrapped to concrete blocks out south of West Ship in sixty feet of water where the dredges don't work. He killed Gibbs. He's dead. You wanted his mouth shut, it's shut. I never got into anything this heavy before. I feel sick when I think about it. What you better do, Tuck, you pray for my good health."

"Because you probably wrote it all down and put it in a safe place?"

"You guess pretty good. I get rid of Jack, so who gets rid of me?"

"Nobody. It never entered my mind."

Mike Wasser stood up and looked down at Tucker Loomis. "We're buddies for life, Tuck. We're stuck with each other. You come on like a smiling shit-kicking good ol' country boy. But I know what you're like on the inside and you know what I'm like. What you should want to do from here on in is keep me fat and happy."

"If I happen to feel like it."

"I want you to feel like it."

"I know. I know. But where's your leverage?"

"I might think of something."

"First thing you think of, find me a new dockmaster, tell him that with those two boys Jack hired, he can keep them or fire them. It'll be his option. But if he wants to hire any, it has to be with your approval. Try to find a better man than we had before. I got complaints about him taking stuff off the boats. Mostly booze."

"He won't be taking any more."

"That would be a real good line in a movie or on the TV. But right now between just us two, it sounds stupid. Plain stupid. You better get on back to work."

"It isn't anything I can just shrug off. I had bad dreams last night, like I could see his white face coming up through the black water instead of going down."

"That's twice you told me the same thing."

"So I'm boring you," Mike said.

"Those two boys down there at the yacht basin, you're damn well sure they both believe I fired Jack and he packed up and took off."

"They believe it."

Tucker Loomis sat on the blue wooden crawl-through and watched big Mike Wasser walk slowly up the green slope to the gate in the wire fencing. He disappeared behind plantings and then Tucker saw him again for a few moments, heading down the road on one of the tractors the maintenance crews used to keep Parklands and the golf course looking trim and elegant. A small cruiser went by and gave him a quick blat on the air horn. He looked and waved. Mrs. Hennesey and her retarded daughter. Bought one of the big places with the money Hennesey made on fast-food franchises before his heart clogged up and quit.

He lifted his fist and started to thump it against the faded blue wood next to him, but the blow landed with a sudden and startling force. He winced and kneaded the edge of his hand. No need to fuss. The wind always blows and the dust always covers everything sooner or later. Hennesey was asleep in his watertight box back there near town at Golden Gates Cemetery, wearing his best suit, asleep now for a year and a half, with no dreams to bother him at all, at all.

RAW DATA—UNEDITED TRANSCRIPT—YODER INTERROGATION

It is ten a.m. on Saturday, September twentieth, and this testimony is being taken in a small banquet room in the West Bay Hyatt Hotel in West Bay, Mississippi. I am D. Porter Mallory, Special Agent in Charge of a team investigating corruption and malfeasance in office in Mississippi, Alabama and Louisiana as directed by the Washington Headquarters of the Federal Bureau of Investigation. Present at this meeting are Albert Junkins, my executive assistant, James Mocinek of the Washington office of the Attorney General of the United States, Harvey Spelling, an attorney with the Bureau, Mrs Helen Yoder who will give testimony, and Mr. Daniel Patrick, Mrs. Yoder's personal attorney. This meeting is being taped. A transcript will be provided to Mrs. Yoder and her attorney for their review and approval. Mrs. Yoder was not subpoenaed. She is a voluntary witness.

MALLORY: Mrs. Yoder, I want you and Mr. Patrick to understand just what this meeting involves. This is an informal questioning. The transcript will most probably be presented to a Grand Jury. The proceedings of the Grand Jury are secret, and will not be released to the press or to anyone else. It may be that the Grand Jury will want to see you in person and ask you additional questions. In view of the fact that you came forward of your own volition, I believe it will be possible to have Mr. Patrick with you should you be called before the Grand Jury. In the event the Grand Jury proceedings result in an indictment, and the prosecution feels there is enough evidence to bring this whole matter to trial, it is possible you will be called as a witness for the prosecution. Questioning at that time will lack the leeway and informality that prevails here. Is that clear?

YODER: Yes, it is.

MALLORY: Will you please describe the events of the night of July eleven and the morning of July twelve, over two months ago. Gentlemen, we will save all questions until she has finished her account.

YODER: At that time I'd been separated from my husband for over a month. He was up in Washington on business, and living with his sister when he was in town. There was a benefit out at the Parklands Yacht Club that night. Buddy, my husband—his name is Hubbard Yoder but he's always been called Buddy—had bought two tickets for us to go to the benefit back in April, I think, when we were still together. The tickets were on my dressing table. They cost a hundred dollars a couple. I had decided not to go, and then on impulse I changed my mind. I felt restless, so I dressed up and went.

It was a buffet dinner and dance. I was put at a table with people I know. We talked and I was asked to dance a few times, and I had a few drinks, and finally I decided to leave by myself and go home. I was tired. The way I left I had to go by the bar, and as I went by, Tucker Loomis called my name. I turned and he came to me and took my hand and led me back to the bar. I had another drink, maybe two, and then he said it was such a nice night it would be fun to go on down the river and out the bay into the Sound in his little boat. And that suddenly seemed to me to be a fine idea. So I agreed.

We went way out, and we anchored in the lee of an island. I found out later it was Bernard Island. We talked about people and old times and so on. I worked for him after my first husband was killed in a one-car accident over five years ago. I was hired to sell some of the lots at Parklands, and I also worked in his office downtown. I was very upset by my husband's death and I was vulnerable, I guess. Anyway I entered into an affair with Mr. Loomis. It wasn't out in the open or anything, but I guess a lot of people knew or suspected. His wife wasn't really well at that time, and now, of course, she is a complete invalid. She can't even talk. She was a Casswell, an old well-to-do family in this area. Anyway, even if she was in the best of health, I think Tuck would be going around chasing women. That's his way.

He opened some wine he had in the little electric cooler. We drank the wine. It was a beautiful night. He had some extra clothes and gear aboard and he loaned me a swimsuit, black and white stripes, a little small for me but not too much. He put on some red trunks. And we went swimming. His boat has a little platform thing on the transom that you can swim from. If I hadn't been drinking I wouldn't have gone in at night. It scares me to go in at night. You can't see what might be in the water nearby. But Tuck was there and I was feeling . . . reckless and foolish. Okay, so after we got back aboard, we started making love. I said no at first and then I said . . . what the hell. W had gone together for almost a year after Cordell Strange, my husband died. It was like . . . for old times' sake.

When I woke up the next morning early, before dawn I guess, I could hear a funny wallowing sloshing sound and I looked out the little port and saw Tuck swimming by. It was lighter when he came below. By then I was in a rotten mood. I had a headache from the wine and I was disappointed in myself for letting him have me and, I guess, for enjoying it. When we broke up I didn't want anything more to do with him because I'd found out he is really a pretty sorry human being. He's ruthless and he's greedy. And sometimes he is cruel. But when he wants to be, he can be good company. So I had broken my word to myself and that made me feel depressed. I didn't even want to talk to him.

The boat was so still I thought maybe we were back at the dock and then I found out we were ten miles out, about a half mile, he said, off Bernard Island. I realized it was Friday and I had morning appointments and I had to get to the office. And I was worried about being conspicuous when we got back to Parklands. The tennis courts aren't far from the little yacht basin, and there I would be in the morning light in a blue cocktail dress getting off Tuck's boat to get to my van. It wasn't that I worried so much about poeple seeing that I'd been out all night with a man, it was because the man was Tucker Loomis.

When we'd gone together before he had a big cruiser, fifty-four feet I think it was, and he had to keep it down in a marina on the bay because it drew too much water to come up the river, and besides he had to avoid all the shallows in the Sound, and when we were going to get the edge of a hurricane he—

SPELLING: Could we stay with the events of that day?

PATRICK: I have Mr. Mallory"s assurance that Mrs. Yoder can tell her story in her own way and in her own good time.

MALLORY: That's correct. Please proceed, Mrs. Yoder.

YODER: Anyway, he could afford a lot bigger boat but he said they were too much trouble and too conspicuous. We used to spend a lot of time together on the big boat, the *Thelma II*, years ago.

I said we had to be getting back but he wouldn't leave and he wouldn't even tell my why he wouldn't leave. He's the sort of person that if you keep questioning him, he gets furious. I took a short swim and then looked through the clothes and found a pink pullover shirt and some white shorts spotted with green paint. He put on old khaki pants and a ragged white shirt.

Finally, after he'd looked at his watch a hundred times, he decided to tell me what was happening. He said that in the next fifteen minutes a man was going to arrive in a float plane. He said he was supposed to be alone on the boat for this meeting, but he said he would feel a lot better about it if he had a witness. That's when I really got mad at the son of a bitch. He'd let me believe it was like some kind of sentimental journey, but what he really wanted was to have a witness aboard. He told me he had planned to bring Mike Wasser along. Mike works for him. But then he saw me at the club and decided I would be more fun than Mike.

He said that as soon as he spotted the plane, he would holler down to me and I should get into the port bunk and way up in the corner against the bulkhead so that anybody looking down below through the open doorway would think it was empty down there. I wasn't to make a sound until Tuck called me, and then I was to come up and meet this man who was coming by air. He said his name was Wilbur Barley and he worked for the government.

He called down and I did as he said and I could hear the plane. It landed and taxied close and I felt the little motion of the boat when the man stepped onto the stern platform. The plane moved away then and the engine stopped. I can't remember the exact words they said to each other. Mr. Barley seemed anxious about whether Tuck had brought "it." He was nervous about being seen with Tuck. And he didn't want to sit down when Tuck asked him. When Tuck said he'd brought along only half, Mr. Barley was angry. He didn't want to go through with it. He said it was too risky. Tuck told him that he had half of it aboard, in hundreds. And I guess that was when he gave it to Mr. Barley. They talked about risk and whether it would work out or wouldn't work out, and if Barley would give the money back if it didn't. That was just Tuck's way, teasing and shoving.

I do remember some of the words Tuck used. He said, "You are going to make damn well sure the U.S. Attorney's Office fumbles the ball real good when we come to trial." And Mr. Barley said he was going to try to do it, but it wasn't easy.

Then Tuck called me and I came out and Tuck introduced us. Mr. Barley jumped up and he got so white and sweaty I thought he was going to faint. He was furious. Tuck told him he didn't have to worry about me. Barley said he hadn't wanted to worry about anybody but Tuck. Tuck said he had two people to worry about, Barley and his pilot. Barley said the pilot was his brother-in-law. Tuck said so the brother-in-law talks to his wife, and Barley said his sister had fallen and hit her head and she was in a coma and had been for a year and a half. And that's why they needed the money. Tuck said that it made him feel better about Barley, knowing he didn't want the money so he could take it to Vegas or Atlantic City.

Well, I was there and there just wasn't anything Mr. Barley could do about it. He had a package in his hand in a brown envelope. He signaled the airplane and it came over and Tuck held a wing while Mr. Barley stepped from the platform to the pontoon and climbed into it. So then we came on home. Tuck seemed real happy about how the meeting had gone. Tuck got my van and drove it down to the dock and I left in my borrowed clothes carrying my blue dress. And that was it.

MOCINEK: Could you describe Mr. Barley?

YODER: I'd guess he was between thirty-five and forty. He was pale and a little bit fat. He combed his blonde hair forward so that he had bangs across his forehead, cut off straight. He had glasses with gold wire rims. He wore white slacks and gray running shoes and a green short-sleeved sport shirt with a gator on the left breast. He wore it tucked into his pants. He wore a brown belt, a dress belt, and it looked wrong with the rest of his outfit. He didn't look as if he was ever outdoors much. Oh, and he had a little pale blonde mustache.

MOCINEK: Can you describe the plane and the pilot?

YODER: The pilot wore a baseball cap and I couldn't read what it said. He had on dark glasses. He was tan and I got the impression he was quite thin. The airplane was mostly white and it had thin light blue stripes on it. There was brown tape on the rudder thing, I guess hiding the numbers.

JUNKINS: How about the envelope?

YODER: Well, it was a brown mailing envelope, the thick paper kind that opens on the wide side and not at the narrow top. It looked as if it had two thick paperback books in it, end to end, and then it was folded over. While the plane was coming back, Mr. Barley pulled his green shirt out of his pants and put the envelope against his stomach and tucked the shirt back in, because he would need two hands to climb into the airplane.

MALLORY: Was any specific amount of money mentioned?

YODER: No. Just that it was in hundreds.

SPELLING: How and why did you get in touch with Mr. Mallory?

YODER: How? Well, I knew of course that Mr. Barnes had been writing a lot of things about the Bernard Island Corporation and the court case, and I knew that he was a good friend of Mr. Rowley, and so I went to Mr. Barnes and introduced myself and asked him how a person would go about getting in touch with the FBI. He said that Mr. Mallory had been in touch with him, and so he gave me the phone number Mr. Mallory had given him.

SPELLING: That leaves the question of why, doesn't it?

PATRICK: I think I object to that tone of voice, Harvey. Helen Yoder appears here voluntarily.

SPELLING: Terribly sorry. But you will ask her to answer the question? I'm always curious about motive.

YODER: He doesn't have to ask me to answer you. I phoned Mr. Mallory because I wanted to. Ever since Tucker was awarded that huge sum of money I've worried about how he fixed it.

SPELLING: You thought it your duty as a citizen?

PATRICK: Porter, please ask your in house attorney over there to back off. Otherwise I am going to advise my client to stop her voluntary testimony about this. She seems to offend his delicate sensibilities.

MALLORY: You hear the man, Harvey.

PATRICK: I happen to know why she decided to appear here. But it is a can of worms you don't want to open.

SPELLING: You can be subpoenaed, Patrick.

PATRICK (laughing): And made to reveal privileged information? Where'd you get your mail-order degree, fellow?

SPELLING: I will not put up with this insolent shit from this—

MALLORY: Spelling, get the hell out of here. Go out to the bar, nurse a beer. Anything. But don't stay here.

SPELLING: My orders are to—

MALLORY: Get out!

YODER: Now that he's gone I guess I really have no good reason to hide why I'm here. I work for a very fine man named Wade Rowley. I'm a successful real estate salesman. I made thirty-seven thousand dollars last year and I'll do a little better this year. My success is due to his patience and direction. Okay? Wade has been trying to extricate the agency from a relationship with Tucker Loomis that his partner, Bernard Gibbs, established. Wade was against the commercialization of Bernard Island. He went to Park Service people and gave them information that four deeds to land on the island were false. The Park Service man sent that data with a letter to the U.S. Attorney's Office. Mr. Barley evidently found out about it and got in touch with Tuck. Then Tuck told Bern Gibbs, and the two partners then had a terrible quarrel and decided to split up. Eleven days ago somebody called and left a message for Wade Rowley to go to the trailer of an employee of Tuck's named Mr. Feeney. Mr. Gibbs intercepted the call and decided to keep the four o'clock appointment. He thought, I guess, that it had something to do with this whole mess, and maybe Wade was being tricky. So he went and he got killed. The coroner's report said that he died of a kick or a blow to the throat that smashed the larynx, and that he had been hit in the face with such force it cracked the jawbone on the left side. It seemed to me that the idea was to lure Wade Rowley to that place and beat him up, to teach him not to mess with Tucker Loomis. Knowing Tuck as I do, I think that would be the sort of thing he would arrange, to send some men there to beat up on Wade. But I guess they didn't know him by sight, and when Bern showed up they beat on him. I called Mr. Mallory because I got the feeling that Tucker might not want to leave a job undone. He's like that. He's very stubborn and he hols grudges. I decided that he would probably wait a couple of months or a year and then send somebody after Wade. He never forgives anybody for anything, ever. That's why I'm here. If I can get him into real trouble, I certainly want to. Bern was not a nice man, really. But he didn't deserve that! Nobody deserves being kicked to death and left in the bushes for a dog to find him.

PATRICK: Gentlemen, let me step in here for a moment. Regardless of what Mrs. Yoder and Mr. Rowley and I might think about Bern Gibbs' death, the local police have closed their file on it. They say the murder was committed by two young men from the Louisiana area who killed Bern to take possession of his forty-thousand-dollar car. They were killed in it in the early hours of the next day over in Alabama trying to run a roadblock.

JUNKINS: What do you think of Mrs. Yoder's account of the killing?

PATRICK: I find it just as plausible as the case against the two young men.

234

MALLORY: Excuse me while I look at my notes. Okay. Now then, Mrs. Yoder, have you heard Tucker Loomis or anyone close to him talking about a company called Maxim Engineering? Or about a buyout?

YODER: No, not that I remember.

MALLORY: Have you heard any mention of Cordray Communications?

YODER: No sir.

MALLORY: Do you know a man named Dennis Short?

YODER: Yes, I do. Not real well. He works for Woody Daggs. Woody owns Regal Construction. He's done a lot of work for Tuck and they are good friends. Buddy, my husband, knows Dennis Short better than I do. They play golf together a lot. I'd say Dennis was the number two man at Regal, after Woody.

MALLORY: Do you know Warner Ellenson?

YODER: He used to be mayor. Everybody knows him. I sold the Ellensons their lot at Parklands.

MALLORY: At the time you were . . . seeing Tucker Loomis, can you recall who his close friends were at that time?

YODER: I've named two of them, Mr. Daggs and Warner Ellenson. J. Harrison Derks, he's president of the Citizens Bank, and Fred Pittman and Colonel Barkis, they're investors in real estate and so on, and they own part of Parklands. Let me see. Sam Loudner, he's an important lawyer. Buddy is in his firm. That's all I can think of. They play golf together and go hunting together and go fishing together and go off to Vegas together. I mean it is an important group of men and there isn't much that can go on in West Bay if they don't approve it.

MALLORY: Does the name Stuart Persons mean anything to you?

YODER: The short time I worked in Tuck's office I had to place calls to him. Out of town someplace. I can't remember where.

MOCINEK: Mrs. Yoder, I am very grateful to you, even though I have heard some things here today which make me very sad indeed. I must ask you a very delicate question, and I hope you understand. In the event this should come to trial and you should be called as a witness, will the defense be able to come up with anything that will discredit you?

YODER: I don't understand what you mean.

MOCINEK: Well, your reputation, your habits?

YODER: You mean can they make me out a drunken slut, like some kind of hooker? I was never unfaithful to Cordell, or to Buddy. If you don't count that night on the boat with Tuck. There was one man for a very short time between Cordell's death and when Tuck hired me. He wasn't married, but he is now. No, I don't get sloppy drunk in public, and I don't screw around. I'm not what you call really well liked, I guess. That's because all my life I've said what I think.

PATRICK: Mrs. Yoder's reputation in West Bay is good.

MOCINEK: What about revenging herself on Loomis for having dropped her years ago?

YODER: Tuck usually doesn't put things in writing, personal things. But he did write me a letter over five years ago and I kept it. He says in the letter he didn't really blame me for breaking up with him, but he was going to miss me a lot, and he wished me happiness.

MALLORY: Just one last thing. I just noticed it here in my notes. Do you know anything about the business relationship between Tom French and Tucker Loomis?

YODER: He used to do a lot of Tuck's real estate work. Tom set up some kind of a limited partnership to invest in raw land. Tuck bought in and then sold out at a profit and the other investors got back maybe a dime on the dollar. It was a big stink and it was investigated but they didn't come up with anything. Since then Tuck hasn't used Tom that I know of.

MALLORY: That's all. Anybody else? No? Thank you, Mrs. Yoder.

MOCINEK: Just one more. Does this Wade Rowley know you contacted Agent Mallory?

YODER: No sir. And I'd just as soon he wouldn't find out. He wouldn't want anybody being that protective about him. Can I ask a question?

MALLORY: Of course

YODER: Are you fixing to nail Tuck?

MALLORY: Don't expect to have it happen tomorrow. Or next month. But expect it to happen. For sure. Count on it.

YODER: Because if you don't, I could be in trouble.

On that same Saturday at four in the afternoon Wade Rowley was working late and alone at the office, trying to reconstruct Bern's expense account for the year up to the date of death, using the random notes and reminders he had found in a top desk drawer, in a file and in a notebook Nita had discovered in Bern's desk at home, along with those charge accounts which had been billed to Bern personally rather than to the business accounts. It was a tiresome, irritating task, and when the phone rang he thought it was Beth asking him how much longer he would be working on a Saturday afternoon.

"Wade? This here is Boob. Boob Davis."

"What can I do for you?"

"Well, we're setting over here in Tuck's office, here in the bank, and we got to talking about you, called your house and Miz Beth give us this number."

"Who's we?"

"Me and Tuck, just the two of us. And Tuck, he was wondering if you'd come on by here, you got a minute."

"What for?"

"I guess Tuck wants to tell you something or ask you something."

"What about?"

"You know how he is. Me, I just work here."

"Is he right there?"

"Yes he is. You want to talk to him?"

"No. You tell him that if he wants to say something to me he can come here, alone, and say it. I'll be here."

"You sound a little bit pissed off, Wade."

"That's a pretty good description. You tell him that."

"Hold on." Wade waited. "Hey, we'll be over pretty soon."

"Just him, Boob," Wade said and hung up.

After the call he could not keep his attention on the task at hand and so he wandered restlessly around the main area of the offices, from desk to desk. The buff-colored Lincoln town car pulled up in front of the door. Tucker Loomis got out on the passenger side leaving Boob behind the wheel. He wore a tweed cap, a gray cardigan, gray slacks. Wade saw him pause, square his shoulders and take a deep breath before coming to the door. Wade met him there and opened the door for him.

"Hey, Wade! Sure glad you can spare me some time."

"Not very much time. And I'm not going to shake hands with you."

"Isn't that a kind of chicken-shit attitude?" Tucker asked, grinning, lowering his hand.

"Probably."

"We going to stand by the door? Come on. Let's sit. I've got some things to say. I want to clear the air."

Wade led him back to Bern's office, sat at Bern's big slab desk and waved Tucker Loomis into the straight chair at the end of the desk.

"This isn't easy," Tucker said.

"Don't expect me to make it easier."

"What's the worst thing you're holding against me, Wade?"

"Sucking Bern into your swindle. I guess that's what really got him killed. Because I owned half the business, it put me in business with you, and I don't like that feeling at all."

Loomis jumped up and began to pace back and forth in front of the desk. He had shoved the tweed cap to the back of his skull. "Let's get right down to that word you used. *Swindle.* I was talking to somebody a while back, and he said the same kind of thing, but not the way you just said it. And I told him and I'm telling you that the thing I wanted to do most was develop Bernard Island into the finest private resort community anywhere on the Gulf of Mexico."

He stopped in front of the desk and frowned at

Wade. "I went out there to the island more than a year ago one fine day, all alone. And I walked to the top of that biggest dune there on the southeast. We'd just done some prelimanry drawings, and from the top of that dune I could see the whole island, and I could see where everything would be, the clubs, the boat basin, the landing pad and all the big houses. One of them was going to be mine, and it was going to be a million-dollar house, maybe designed by somebody like that I.M. Pei fellow. I could see the plantings and the beaches and I stood up there and I tell you for sure, and I'm not funnin' you, I felt like the king of that island. That's what I wanted to do."

"Bullshit, Tuck. You knew then you could never get all the permissions you'd have to have. You knew then that every few years storm surges go right over those islands out there. And you knew then that sooner or later the Park Service was going to buy that island. You knew from your contracts it was on their priority list."

Tuck leaned both fists on the desk. "Now just who the hell are you to say bullshit to me? If all my life I listened to every wimp that told me something couldn't be done, I'd still be piddling around building shacky little houses one at a time. I *could* get the permissions. Structures *can* be built to withstand storm surges and hurricane winds. Want to guess how many people told me Parklands would be a failure?"

"Maybe you're just one of those people who can make themselves believe whatever is convenient at the time. Whatever you say or I say, we both know the swindle worked. But maybe you'll lose on appeal."

Loomis sighed and went back to the chair. "Not a chance. We'll have the complete transcript. We made our case and they'll pay us."

"If your idea was so wonderful, why did you have to sign up fake purchasers, and order Bern to screw up our office records here? Why did you have to set somebody on me to beat me up?"

"Who said that?"

"A man named Feeney."

For long seconds there was no expression on Tucker's face. Then he gave a quick shrug and said, "Let's get down to that. Word come back to me that somebody had given copies of the four mortgage deeds to the Park Service, which gave them to the U.S. Attorney. First I had to find out it wasn't any of my people doing it, and it wasn't. Strange as it may seem to you, Rowley, I get a lot of loyalty from my people and from the people I do business with. And I did some loud bitching about the leak and about you, because by then I knew and Bern knew it had to be you holding our nuts over the fire. So I figured out later that somebody that works for me, trying to do me a favor, they tried to lure you to Feeney's place and work you over. And they got Bern instead."

"What people?"

"Now I wouldn't know that, would I? I mean, it's not as if I gave anybody any orders. Hell, I never got to know you real well, Wade, but I know you enough to realize that bumping you around would just turn you into more of a nuisance than you were already."

Who do you think did it?"

"Did exactly what? Let's be careful here."

"Killed Bern."

"I think it was those Mex kids that come along at the right time to take the car. He was hurt some and they finished him off."

"Okay, who do you think hurt him some?"

"I couldn't be sure of that. I had one man took off sudden, but he could have had other reasons. I wouldn't want to say. All I can say is that if any of my people had anything to do with it, I want to tell you how sorry I am. Bern was a big loss to me personally, as I know he was to you. At the funeral there I tried to get through the crowd to tell you that, but you were gone before I could get to you."

"I made sure I was gone before you could get to me. I wasn't sure of what I'd do or try to do if you tried to speak to me. And I still don't know what I'm doing talking to you at all."

"Did Bern tell you about the future plans for Parklands?"

"I remember him telling me that if you lost out on the case due to anything I did, you were going to make sure that no bank in this area would ever touch a real estate deal where this agency was involved."

Tucker laughed and shook his head. "You had to be there, Wade. Hell, I get mad quick and I get over it quick. I say things before I think. And Bern, you know, he tended to be edgy. Nervous about things. About money and all."

"And you're not?"

"If you think too hard about money, it stays away from you. I think about projects, how things are going to look."

"Why are you here? What do you want?"

"Just to clear the air. That's all. I'm human. It bothers me to have somebody hating me because they don't get the whole picture. You and me, whether you can believe this or not, we could work together pretty good. One of these days I'd like to listen to how you'd plan out my extra acreage at Parklands, and how you'd handle the sale of it."

"For God's sake, Tuck!"

"Now don't jump too fast. There's a lot of money out there for the both of us. You've got a good head on you. And—"

"Hold it a minute! Let me think this out so I will be able to say it just right. Now I think I've got it. I want to make sure you understand me. I will not go into any kind of business relationship with you, ever. I will never eat at a table with you. I will never walk down a street with you. I will never shake your hand. For all practical purposes, to me you are just as dead as Bern."

For a moment something seemed to move behind Tucker's eyes, something cold, ancient, reptilian. And then he got up and walked out and closed the door gently behind him. The Lincoln moved away without a sound.

Boob Davis arrived at twenty to six just as Wade was setting the security system. He arrived in a rental Pontiac and told Wade he'd asked Tuck to drop him off, and he said he wanted to talk for a few minutes. Maybe they could talk in his car.

So Wade got into the rental, into a smell of newness and cigars. He had known Boob most of his life, liked

244

him, did not think he wanted to trust the man. Boob was that rare bird, a man *so* likeable that some other men were wary of him.

"Well, you didn't exactly make a close buddy for life," Boob said.

"And you're here to fix the damage?"

"Shit, no! It can't be fixed and you don't want it fixed."

"What the hell was on his mind anyway?"

"You're not that dumb, Wade. Ol' Tuck, he's feeling a little slippage here and there. He wants to snuggle up to respectability, that's all. He's been stroking people all day, made a few points here and there. Struck out a lot too."

"So what do *you* want?"

"Put you in a mood, didn't he? Hey, this is old Boob Davis here talking to his old fishing buddy."

"Old fishing buddy, you work for a man I despise. I don't trust him and that means I can't trust you either. He sucked Bern in and threw him away. So if you've got a point to make, you better stop stalling. I've got to get home."

"This isn't the right time or place but I got the feeling it is the only time and place I am going to get. I don't have to tell you what I've been doing. I've been putting together deals for Tuck for a lot of years now. Chasing them down. Sweet-talking them out of their hidey-holes. Real good money and lots of fun."

"You going to quit?"

"I just don't know yet. Let me say that it's a possibility. A couple of things have happened that I feel kinda strange about. And somehow they seem to come up in conversation here and there. They are the kind of things that when people talk about them, then you start to get this slippage I talked about. And a man like Tuck, you give that kind of a man too much slippage, he hasn't got the patience to wait it out and build back. He wants to do something right now, and he could get so upset it could be a real dumb thing. You follow?"

"Yes I do. You after advice?"

"Not exactly. You know, I kid around. I get a lot of laughs. I'm good old Boob Davis. But in my own way I make things happen."

"I know you do."

"And I make pretty good guesses. My guess right now is that when somebody starts to cut down the tree I'm roosting in, I want to have another tree in mind. Like for example I see how many shares in your candy store one hundred big ones will buy, and then as a minority shareholder, I smoke out deals for Rowley/ Gibbs, no salary, just commission. I've got a broker's license, you know. Don't get to use it."

"Talk to me next week."

"Is there any chance at all?"

"Of buying in? None. Of any other arrangement? A very small maybe. It would depend on...a lot of things."

"With Tuck, I was never into any of the real gummy stuff."

"I believe you."

'And you've already forgot I talked to you like this."

"Sure have," Wade said, getting out of the car.

* * *

A year ago they had moved the regular poker session to a special card room. Tuck had built onto the east wing of the Parklands Golf and Country Club.

They met at the bar between eight and eight-thirty on Saturday nights and broke up about twelve-thirty. It was usually an interesting game but not a big money game. It was table stakes, pot limit, a dollar ante. There were usually seven, sometimes six, and each man started with fifty dollars in chips. If he went broke he could put up another fifty between deals, but not during a hand.

Tucker Loomis was at the bar at quarter to eight. He'd finished half a drink when a call came in and Timmy the bartender put the phone in front of him. It was Woody Daggs. "Hey, Tuck? Look, old buddy, I won't be able to make it tonight. Something came up. And Sam asked me to tell you to count him out too."

"That cuts it down to five. Makes it kind of tight."

"Well, I'm real sorry about that. But you know how it goes. Some days you can't make a dime."

At eight o'clock it was a call from Warner. "Awful goddamn sorry, Tuck, but I got to cancel out tonight. Sorry to be so late letting you know. There's something I have to straighten out, down in town."

At eight-fifteen Pink Derks called and said he had a fever of a hundred and two and his wife had ordered him to stay the hell home before he got worse and gave it to the other guys.

Colonel Barkis arrived with a message from Fred Pittman. Fred had to stay home and wait for a call from his daughter in Boston. She was having some kind of trouble.

They sat side by side on the bar stools. "That cuts it down to two," Tuck said. "Want to play gin?"

"I don't think so, thanks."

"Real strange, everybody pooping out like this. I don't think it ever happened before, not that I can remember. One time we played with five. But down to two! Jesus! What's going on?"

"What do you mean?"

"Are the boys tired of the game or something, Colonel?"

"I wouldn't know,," the Colonel said. He looked at his watch. "I think I better be getting along. Thanks for the drink."

"You're welcome."

The Colonel looked at Tuck. "By the way, I think I better tell you now, I'm going to be otherwise engaged for the next two Saturday nights. I probably better give you a ring when I'm free."

Looking into the Colonel's ice blue eyes Tucker suddenly got the message. He didn't know how it had happened or why it had happened, but the message was quite clear.

"Yes, you do that. When you're free."

Timmy came over. "Looks like the game is off?"

"I think the game is over."

"What?"

"Never mind."

"What'll I tell the kitchen about the snacks, Mr. Loomis?"

"Tell them to take the snacks and—" He brought

himself back under control. "We won't be needing them tonight. If they're all made, put them on my account and leave them here on the bar for anybody who wants some. Good night."

Tucker Loomis walked out into the cool and pleasant night. He had the feeling that he was in some kind of spacetime dislocation, standing a little bit apart from himself. He had walked down to the club and so he started to walk home. He remembered a time long ago when he had felt exactly like this.

He had been at the Sands in Las Vegas playing one of the crap tables. For long hours his luck had been uncertain, and he had made money slowly and carefully by playing the odds, playing the field, betting with the hot shooter, passing the dice when they came to him. It was dog work. When your luck is bad, you walk away from it and come back another day. When it is good, you push it. When it hangs dead, you do the best you can, five dollars at a time.

Quite suddenly, at one in the morning, the luck had come flowing back. He was with a shooter on a six, then an eight, then a ten, then a four, had bet against the shooter when he crapped, and then again when he sevened out trying to make a nine.

When the dice came to him, he knew he was going to make some passes. He felt it. He didn't know how many. He bounced the dice hard off the far end of the table. A seven. Then a six which he made with a pair of threes. A seven. An eleven. An eight which he made with a six deuce. He'd started his roll with a hundred dollars and had let it ride. Two hundred, four hundred, eight hundred, sixteen hundred, thirty-two hundred. Seven! Sixty-four hundred. When he wanted to let it ride, the pit boss came over and approved it, and then stood by to watch the action. He rolled a four, and after five more rolls made the four. Twelve thousand eight.

The smart thing to do would be to drag the twelve and shoot eight hundred. He shook the dice, thinking. The pit boss approved the roll for the whole pile. He still hesitated. And then he could see with great clarity what the dice were going to do. He could see them against the green felt, brighter than life, with sharper edges. A six and a one. And then he would drag twenty-five thousand and go to bed.

With total confidence he rolled the dice, rolled them hard. They whacked the far end of the table and came tumbling back, and he was smiling in anticipation. Six and six. Boxcars. Busted.

He could not remember leaving the casino floor and going outside. It was a clear cool night then also. A woman tugged at him, mumbling her dirty words, and he shoved her away.

He had felt confused and helpless then as he did now. Life had bounced and rolled and it had come up wrong again. For absolutely no reason.

He suddenly realized he was back home. He unlocked the door and went in. He startled Shirley, the nurse. He had told her he wouldn't be back until after Mrs. Madigan had relieved her. Thelma was asleep. He went in and stood by her bed. It was so still he could hear her breathing. He wondered what moved through her dreams, what stirred in her world without words.

He went back through the darkened house to his study, turned on the desk light, opened the safe in the closet and took out a rectangular box covered with dark blue fabric. The two latches were ivory pins which slid into little leather loops.

He opened it under the desk lamp and looked at the ten Masanao *netsuke*, each in its open compartment lined with white silk. He took the delicate masterpieces out one at a time and aligned them on the green blotter under the bright desk light with its green shade. Ancient ivory, with tiny age cracks and glossy patina. A seated hare, a monkey with a persimmon, a Kirin, a Shishi, a fat young dog, a swimming carp, a stylized sparrow, a standing figure of Fukurokuju, a grazing pony and the rat so recently purchased at auction in London.

He remembered where and when and how each piece had been acquired. He knew the provenance of each piece, the name of the previous collector. Davey, Meinertzhagen, Sharpe, Ford, Murakami, Hepworth. Each piece had been authenticated.

He handled them, trying to rekindle the pleasure of possession, trying to imagine once again what it would be like to present this small and superb collection to one of the great museums.

But he could not respond. Not this time. He replaced them in the box and noticed just as he closed it that he had them in the wrong order. But he did not rearrange them. He replaced them in the safe with the feeling that it might be a long time before he would take them out again. It might be forever.

He went out into the night and walked down near the river and sat as before in the children's playground, on the blue wooden crawl-through. The cool wind came off the river. He rocked slowly from side to side and made a small humming sound in his throat.

14

Sunday morning. The twenty-first day of September. A cold front had come bulging down out of Canada, all the way through Kansas, Missouri, Oklahoma, Arkansas and Louisiana, all the way to the top of the Gulf of Mexico. It was the first of the season, changing the long hot days to an anticipation of winter.

Maria arrived ten minutes early to relieve Mrs. Madigan, and they talked in the kitchen about the sudden cold spell, and reaching for blankets in the night and how long and hot and dry the summer and early fall had been. A deficit of nearly twelve inches of rain, they said. No hurricanes had come booming in this year to soak the land, not like last year with four of them.

Mrs. Madigan said their patient seemed the same as usual. Possibly she had a little cold starting. They would have to be careful of that. In her condition a cold could turn quickly to pneumonia.

After Mrs. Madigan drove out, Maria looked in on Mrs. Loomis and then tiptoed along the hall and opened Tuck's door and saw him sound asleep on his back, snoring with each deep slow inhalation, popping his lips with each exhalation. She closed the door and went back and stood at the foot of the bed and looked at Thelma Loomis. Thelma looked back. First the bed pan to avoid the sodden chore of changing the whole bed. The woman's nostrils and eyelids looked slightly red. After Maria had emptied and rinsed the bed pan, she stood at the foot of the bed again.

She had a sudden thought. It made her heart bump in her chest and it made her breath shallow. She stood and thought about it and then decided to do it. She folded the blanket and the sheet down to the foot of the bed. She went to the window and unlatched it and turned the crank that opened the three big glass panels, opened them to the horizontal. The north breeze blew in, dank and chilly. She looked at her watch. She avoided looking again at the woman's face, not wanting to look into her eyes.

She went quickly to Tuck's room and undressed and slipped in beside him, nuzzling her face into his neck, shivering a little, running her spread fingers through the wiry thatch of gray hair on his big broad chest. He held her in his big arms. His breath was sour. When he did not respond, she ducked down under the bedding to arouse him. She kept thinking of Thelma in the cold wind. It scared her and excited her to think of the woman. It made her anxious to get Tuck ready to take her.

Tuck lay on his back, eyes closed, feeling the soft manipulative pressures. Cool sunlight was bright against the windows. It shone through his eyelids, a pink glow. He thought about the sun and wondered how deep the light would shine in the waters of the Gulf off the Ship Islands. He seemed to see all the way down to the bottom of that anchorage, a sandy bottom where Jack Simms, enchained, rolled over and back, over and back, in a tidal current. He could see him so clearly in the faint sunlight down there he could see the familiar faded tattoo on Jack's bicep. Eagle and flag and seal. Semper Fidelis. Meaning, as Jack always said, "Fuck you, buddy. I've got mine." And in the faint submarine glow he could see the silver flickering of a school of small predatory fish as they darted about the body.

He sat up abruptly and pushed her away from him. She rose up, the bedding caped around her shoulders, eyes wide. "What the hell, Tuck!"

"Just get away from me."

"What's the matter?"

"I can't make it. Not today. Get away from me."

"Let me try some more."

"Can't you understand English, you dumb spic bitch?"

"Who the hell do you think you are?"

"Get your clothes on and get out."

He saw the tears on her cheeks as she dressed. He heard her snuffle. It was emotion without any meaning to him, as though he had turned on the television in the middle of a playlet and somebody was crying and he would never know why. Her arms were too skinny and she was sway-backed, and the left breast hung lower than the right. He wondered why he had been so attracted. But in another part of his mind he was telling himself that it was always like this. All of a sudden it was over and then everything about them was wrong, from their damn dumb expressions to their empty jabber to the smell of their bodies.

He knew she would take another shot at it tomorrow and the answer would be the same. And then if she was bright enough, she would have the message loud and clear. And probably quit and be replaced by a battle-ax like Madigan and like Shirley. A matched set.

Sunday noon. Wade had been dubious about the fishing trip and picnic when he had awakened and seen the change in the weather. With that wind direction it would be fairly calm near shore but kicking up pretty good out by the islands. But his group had been insistent. He found out from the weather station on the cable that the wind was expected to diminish throughout the day.

Six people made a pretty good load for the old Whaler. But Nita and Lois and Kim were all undersized. Tod was already man-size, taller than Beth, with probably two more years of growing to do.

Once they got out to white water, Wade throttled way back. But it was still exhilarating. The bow lifted and fell, whacking up spray that blew forward, away from them. He had selected Bernard Island partly because of the little hook-shaped lagoon near the east end of it that would make a quiet place to pull the boat up on the beach, and partly because it was going to be forever free from development. None of the Tuck Loomises of the world would grab it, ever.

The island was narrow there, and Wade guessed it would be quiet and pleasant on the south side, and so they walked through the trees carrying the picnic basket, ice chest, tackle boxes and spinning rods. On the way through the woods they spooked a pair of rabbits, and it was Lois who spotted the raccoon up in the crotch of a pine.

Tod had dug up a few sand fleas on the north beach, and the three of them, Wade and Tod and Kim, had cast in hopes of attracting the attention of a passing pompano. Kim tired of it and went back along the beach to help set up the picnic.

Wade had intercepted one of the glances Lois Gibbs had given his son, and the naked adoration in that look had startled him.

"How's Nita coming along?" Wade asked.

"I don't know."

"You've been over there enough."

"Is there something wrong with that?"

"Hey! Don't be so damn prickly, boy. I'm not accusing you of a thing. I was wondering about Nita."

"I'm sorry. When I said I don't know, I really don't. She's nice to me. She smiles and talks and so on. But it's like . . . this maybe sounds dumb, but it's like somebody crouched down and holding up a dummy in front of them, a dummy that smiles and talks and does the right things. Like she isn't really *there*."

"I think that's very perceptive. What does Lois say about her mother?"

"Lois is an absolutely wonderful human being."

"Of course. But what does she say?"

"She says her mother is having a hard time."

"Except you're a little edgy lately, you seem to have got past your hard times. What was going on anyway?"

"Well, what was bothering me was so damn dumb and silly and pointless I don't ever think about it anymore."

"Or talk about it?"

"Not ever."

"I'll settle for that. Glad to have you back in one piece."

"Glad to be back," Tod said, grinning. At that moment something hit his bait as he was working it back in, stripped off fifty feet of line and went free.

"Like I hooked into a whale," he said, awed.

"I smell groceries," Wade said, reeling in.

"I hear music."

"If your sister is going to play those tapes of hers, you three kids can take your rations a half mile down the beach."

"Isn't it a beautiful day, Dad?"

"I never knew you noticed."

They walked back to the group. The sun was overhead and the day was getting warmer. Beth smiled at them as she saw them coming, and he knew what was in her heart. It was as if he had a sudden gift of special sight. Kim turned the volume dial down on her boom box and laughed and he knew what she was thinking and knew how she felt. Nita smiled too, and he saw through the smile to bleakness and regret, to a self-awareness of loneliness to come, and even down to a little stain of envy—a jealousy of the two-ness of Wade and Beth. He saw the way Lois looked at Tod, and he knew something about them which he had only begun to suspect. He pushed it out of his mind. Eavesdropping was an uncomfortable habit. He hoped this random ability to see into heads and hearts would fade quickly. It made him uneasy. Let people be people. Cherish them, and trust them to tell you what they think you have a right to know.

Bern, I think you are slowly turning back into the friend you used to be as opposed to the man you became. And I welcome that. It is easier to live with. Now you have left me a pair of shipwrecked women, castaways when your ship went down. So please be aware, my friend, I am going to give it my best shot.

He looked south. The wind out of the north, once it was past the islands, began to pick up the seas, and far far out, the horizon was jagged. Better to be here than there. Here on the sunny beach like a tribal family from long ago, vulnerable to all the forces of the world.

About the Author

John D. MacDonald was graduated from Syracuse University and received an MBA from the Harvard Business School. He and his wife Dorothy, had one son and several grandchildren. Mr. MacDonald died in December 1986.